A WINDOW
IN THRUMS

J. M. BARRIE

Introduced by

IAN CAMPBELL

THE SALTIRE SOCIETY

A Window in Thrums published 2005 by

The Saltire Society
9 Fountain Close,
22 High Street,
Edinburgh EH1 1TF

A catalogue record for this book is available
from the British Library.

ISBN 0 85411 084 4

Scottish
Arts Council

The publisher is very grateful to the Scottish Arts Council
for financial assistance in the publication of this book

Cover Design by James Hutcheson
The photograph of J. M. Barrie (1888) is used
by kind permission of Getty Images.

Printed and Bound in Scotland by Bell and Bain Limited

Contents

INTRODUCTION

A window in Thrums? Well, yes, in a sense Barrie's collection of short stories is a window of sorts on a Scottish village of sorts. And a hugely successful collection, growing from an original ambition to crack the London newspaper market with short pieces developed from his own childhood memories of Kirriemuir, soon supplemented by those his mother sent in response to his urgent appeals for more material. The stories Barrie organised into a book-form collection (he was never short of commercially astute ideas) and this is the result. Long referred to, often derided as kailyard by those who had probably not read a word of them, *A Window in Thrums* is a collection which badly needs to be republished — and read — if Barrie is to have the sort of critical attention he is increasingly receiving.

Kailyard is a word we often hear today, in a blurred sense which needs to be sharpened up. As an all-purpose term of abuse, it serves to delineate a literary movement which peaked at the end of the nineteenth century and the early decades of the twentieth, but whose values have not been altogether superseded by the sharper-edged renaissance of Scottish writing in our own times, by politically committed, doggedly realistic, modern and postmodern writing about a 'real' Scotland. For Kailyard was about a real Scotland too, and *A Window in Thrums* is a key document in understanding the paradoxical nature of that Kailyard Scotland. And the opening chapters are a key in themselves.

> Into this humble abode I would take any one who cares to accompany me. But you must not come in a contemptuous mood, thinking that the poor are but a stage removed from beasts of burden, as some cruel writers of these days say; nor will I have you turn over with your foot the shabby horse-hair chairs that Leeby kept so speckless, and Hendry weaved for years to buy, and Jess so loved to look upon.

i

I speak of the chairs, but if we go together into the "room" they will not be visible to you. For a long time the house has been to let. Here, on the left of the doorway, as we enter, is the room without a shred of furniture in it except the boards of two closed-in beds. The flooring is not steady, and here and there holes have been eaten into the planks. You can scarcely stand upright beneath the decaying ceiling. Worn boards and ragged walls, and the rusty ribs fallen from the fireplace, are all that meet your eyes, but I see a round, unsteady, wax-cloth-covered table, with four books lying at equal distances on it. There are six prim chairs, two of them not to be sat upon, backed against the walls, and between the window and the fireplace a chest of drawers, with a snowy coverlet. On the drawers stands a board with coloured marbles for the game of solitaire, and I have only to open the drawer with the loose handle to bring out the dambrod. In the carved wood frame over the window hangs Jamie's portrait; in the only other frame a picture of Daniel in the den of lions, sewn by Leeby in wool. Over the chimney-piece with its shells, in which the roar of the sea can be heard, are strung three rows of birds' eggs. Once again we might be expecting company to tea.

Here is the author establishing not only his own personality but his own position next to his text — and his readers. And straightway, making a point which people have obstinately failed to take on board in condemning these stories as escapist fantasies. "I speak of the chairs, but if we go together into the 'room' they will not be visible to you." And making another point: "Once again we might be expecting company to tea." That "we" is to be a crucial element in Barrie's story-telling here. For at a stroke, he has mapped out a complicated game between himself as author/rememberer (seeing things we cannot) and his readers (depending on him to re-enter a vanished Scotland) and the game is further complicated by the idea that "we" can still be part of that vanished Scotland. Plainly, those who demanded kailyard fiction wanted that illusion. Barrie, Crockett, Ian Maclaren and a host of lesser kailyarders gave their Scottish readers access to a vanished, lamented, loved county which was still within reach of memory to many, and only just beyond to more. At the same time, they gratified the wishes of many exiled readers (for they were widely read in countries with huge emigrant populations) and gratified the wishes of many more who had never seen Scotland for themselves, but who imagined the place through the illustrated newspapers and through the colossally successful writings of Scott and many other authors. In this Thrums, Barrie the author/narrator/rememberer invites us to tea. Millions were glad to accept.

This taking of a position is at once the collection's strength and its potential weakness. Robert Louis Stevenson, most acute of critics, was quick to spot the weakness: "... Barrie is a beauty, the *Little Minister* and *A Window in Thrums*, eh? Stuff in that young man, but he must see and not be too funny. Genius in him, but there's a journalist at his elbow — there's the risk." [1] The journalist saw the commercial possibilities in the form: the genius would have to control it. Cairns Craig has remarked on the strain between the two sides of Barrie's character,

> This strange ambivalence between the narrator and his subject matter accounts for much of the tone of Barrie's writing, for the narrator, as superior, educated, worldly commentator, submits the community to our scrutiny as an object of mockery for its narrow-minded parochialism, for its strange rituals and unrelieved backwardness; at the same time, however ... the narrator becomes the voice of a lingering nostalgia for a lost sense of community based on religious commitments that have ceased to have any validity to Barrie's audience. [2]

Certainly Barrie's is the educated outsider's voice. The social values he speaks for — the recognition of the poverty of the furniture, the attitude to the poor of Scotland in the mid-nineteenth century — are as resolutely outside the community as is his habit of glossing unfamiliar Scottish words and phrases for the reader's benefit. But has the reader lost all contact with the values of the community? At the close of the nineteenth century, to be sure, the monolithic values of Presbyterian Scotland were in decline, and the picture of small-town Christianity in Thrums and in Ian

Maclaren's Logiealmond was declining in validity. The Free Kirk and the Established Kirk might still frown at one another across the village square, but the reunion of 1929 was decades away, and both would still command much more respect — and weekly attendance — in the small-town environments of Angus and Perthshire than they would have in the cities. And Barrie's audience, however unevenly, was there (and in the distant Presbyterian communities of Canada and the USA) as well as in the post-Christian areas of the cities. As much as Dickens' portraits of the uneven and unpredictable nature of the moral geography of mid-Century London[3], Barrie is aware of the seismic shift of his times, the contrast between the world of London which James inhabits after leaving Thrums and his parents' enduring values. The schoolmaster in his lonely cottage up the glen is isolated in a way parallel to Barrie' s own isolation as narrator/observer: the journalist and the professional writer is aware of the taste of his times clashing uneasily in such a passage as "The last night! Reserve slipped unheeded to the floor. Hendry wandered ben and but the house, and Jamie sat at the window holding his mother's hand. You must walk softly now if you would cross that humble threshold. I stop at the door. Then, as now, I was a lonely man, and when the last night came the attic was the place for me." Where *A Window in Thrums* is at its deftest is where it resists the temptation to milk a scene, where the narrative slips away and leaves the characters to themselves: reticence is his strongest weapon. Cynthia Asquith might be thought to have known Barrie better than most, yet even she responded with puzzlement to the enigma of who he was.

> I knew far too little about him, and his. What *did* I know? I had heard that he had come from a small Scottish town nearly five hundred miles from London, and that this town was the 'Thrums' of his books; that his father had been a weaver in the days of the hand-loom; and his mother the Margaret Ogilvy he had made world-famous by the book of that name. I'd been told, too, that some time in the early 'eighties he had come, penniless and unknown, to London to try to earn a living by

his pen; and that, after two or three years' struggle as a free-lance journalist, he had begun to make a fortune by his books and plays. Beyond that, I had heard nothing except rumours of an unhappy marriage, now broken up, and what I'd just been told about the five adopted boys.[4]

A Window in Thrums obviously contains material arising from experience and from personal hurt: where Barrie is successful, it is through channelling that into well-narrated credible short fictions about characters who seem realistic enough to be believed by those who have never personally known the circumstances of mid-century Thrums. Where Barrie's success wavers is where he milks the story too hard: as one commentator remarked acidly, "James Matthew Barrie could never tell a good story once. This is more than the tactic of the freelancer, Mr. Anon, who is paid by the word and who subtitles his pieces for the extra pence. . . Each story is to be milked until there's nothing left, nothing is to be wasted or thrown away. Hence, we get repetitions and permutations . . . Better if Barrie had relied on his inventiveness rather than reaching into a bag of old tricks"[5]

An old bag of tricks? Hardly. As short stories, these work excellently one at a time, and *A Window in Thrums* has long been a popular book for dipping into. As a framed collection of stories by an implied narrator re-visiting a vanished Scotland, and re-creating it for a mixed audience, the collection as a whole is magnificently successful. As a highly commercial product, pressing the right buttons (reunion, deathbed, family strife and its resolution, piety challenged and affirmed, small-town values challenged and affirmed, friendship, love, marriage) *A Window in Thrums* not only made good reading but it made *acceptable* reading. That it overlooked a great deal of Scotland (and the world) outside Thrums and Thrums values hardly mattered, since the author had adroitly sidestepped that problem in his opening presentation of a world which only he can see: that the author is a kindly voice makes that vanished world acceptable to all, even to those who relish the acidic tone of *The House with the Green Shutters* which, in 1901, revolutionised the genre of reminiscent fiction with its scathingly negative picture of the same narrator. "In every little Scotch community there is a distinct type known as the 'bodie'. . . The chief occupation of his idle hours (and his hours are chiefly idle) is the discussion of his neighbour's affairs. He is generally an 'auld residenter'". Barrie's "auld residenter" (significantly) is one who has moved away and sees his community in memory and with a widened perspective: Brown's residenters stay in their little village and the result is a shockingly narrowed perspective.

> There is a megalomaniac in every parish in Scotland. Well, not so much as that; they're owre canny for that to be said of them. But in every district, almost, you may find a poor creature who for thirty years has cherished a great scheme by which he means to revolutionize the world's commerce, and amass a fortune in monstrous degree. He is generally to be seen shivering at the Cross, and (if you are a nippy man) you shout carelessly in going by, 'Good morning, Tamson; how's the scheme?' And he would be very willing to tell you, if only you would wait to listen . . .

No one could have called the narrator of *A Window in Thrums* a nippy man. His tone made the book a huge commercial success; it infuriated authors of George Douglas Brown's generation and embittered the tone of *The House with the Green Shutters*, a book Brown admitted had "too much black for the white in it", but one he regarded as more "honest" than merely retrospective kailyard.

So what do we make of *A Window in Thrums* re-opening it in the twenty-first century? Disarmed by the opening (and closing) sections, we find it hard to accuse the book of flaccid escapism into a vanished but secure country which is all too typical of second-rate kailyard writing. At the same time, we admit that the values the book respects and represents — Christian, family, secure and unthreatening values existed in Barrie's childhood and continued in some form in his manhood, however partial and incomplete and unthreatening a picture he painted of them. One of the weaknesses of knee-jerk criticism of the kailyard is that the Scotland it represented did, in some measure, exist.

But the strength of such criticism lies in the partial, incomplete, out-of-date nature of the representation of Scotland in much kailyard. And here *A Window in Thrums* stands open to much criticism. Leeby, Hendry, Jess and the shadowy narrator are undeniably well drawn, the other villagers less in focus, the world beyond the railway junction and nearer the distant Edinburgh and London all but unrecognised. Social change, any threat to the established values of an essentially conservative rural economy, any disturbance of Church harmony (or indeed Church power), any redistribution of wealth or power, any suggestion that the women of Thrums might merit a more rewarding existence than they seem to enjoy, any suggestion of reform of the educational system as it stands— these are simply irrelevances to the book. They may be hinted at ("you must not come in a contemptuous mood, thinking that the poor are but a stage removed from beasts of burden, as some cruel writers of these days say") — but the theme is simply not pursued.

Eventually this very reservation was to doom *A Window in Thrums* to the secondhand bookshops, and in part to doom Barrie himself to a kind of shadowy half-life as Kailyard exemplar, often cited as a second-rater, rarely read, still more rarely looked at as a whole, where the early kailyard work takes its place in an enormous, skilful and constantly evolving talent. Fortunately Barrie is now receiving that sort of critical attention.[6] Fortunately also, *A Window in Thrums* has been rescued from the secondhand shops now, and its artistry can be appreciated as well as its shortcomings. To read it is to admire, once more, the clear-sighted critical eye of Stevenson who saw in Barrie's youthful cleverness the seeds of one of Scotland's most intriguing and prolific recent authors.

Ian Campbell
Edinburgh,
November 2004

REFERENCES

1 Quoted in Andrew Birkin, *J M Barrie and the Lost Boys* (London, 1986 ed), p.18.

2 Cairns Craig, *The Modern Scottish Novel* (Edinburgh, 1999), p.59; See also *Out of History* (Edinburgh, 1996), p.57-8.

3 Think of the Milveys and Betty Higden, Jenny Wren's fierce protectiveness of her father and Lizzie Hexam's attitudes to the Jewish paper makers (and Riah) in *Our Mutual Friend* to have some indication of the complexity of mid-century English views of old-fashioned religious values; they were still strongly operative, if uneven, in Scottish cities well into the twentieth century, and much of Thrums' Christian life would have seemed quite recognisable, and quite normal, to readers from such city existence.

4 Cynthia Asquith, *Portrait of Barrie* (London, 1954) 12-13

5 Thomas J Murray, *J M Barrie and the Search for Self* (Harvard PhD 1988), p. 180 (copy in National Library of Scotland).

6 Most notably from R D S Jack, in his *The Road to the Never Land* (Aberdeen, 1991), in much publication since, and in substantial critical work now in preparation. For further reading see also the work by Cairns Craig cited above, Jean Berton, "Que voir de la fenêtre de pennes de J. M. Barrie?" *Cahiers victoriens et edouardiens* 54 (Oct, 2001), 48-62, Elizabeth Waterston, *Rapt in Plaid: Canadian Literature and Scottish Tradition* (Toronto, 2001), and Ian Campbell, "George Douglas Brown's Kailyard Novel", *Studies in Scottish Literature* XII, 1 (July, 1974), 62-73, *Kailyard* (Edinburgh, 1981), "Knowles of Galt (1868-1944)", *Scottish Tradition* XI/XII (1981-2), 163-76, and "A Window on Thrums" in *Studies in Scottish Fiction: the Nineteenth Century* ed. H. W. Drescher and J. Schwend (Lang: Frankfurt and Bern, 1986), 307-20. More recently an important article on this question, a critical discussion of the kailyard and Barrie's relation to it, appeared in *Scottish Studies Review* (5,1, Spring 2004) by Andrew Nash, "William Robertson Nicoll, the Kailyard Novel and the Question of Popular Culture" (pp. 57-73).

Chapter 1

THE HOUSE ON THE BRAE

On the bump of green round which the brae twists, at the top of the brae, and within cry of T'nowhead Farm, still stands a one-storey house, whose whitewashed walls, streaked with the discoloration that rain leaves, look yellow when the snow comes. In the old days the stiff ascent left Thrums behind, and where is now the making of a suburb was only a poor row of dwellings and a manse, with Hendry's cot to watch the brae. The house stood bare, without a shrub, in a garden whose paling did not go all the way round, the potato pit being only kept out of the road, that here sets off southward, by a broken dyke of stones and earth. On each side of the slate-coloured door was a window of knotted glass. Ropes were flung over the thatch to keep the roof on in wind.

Into this humble abode I would take any one who cares to accompany me. But you must not come in a contemptuous mood, thinking that the poor are but a stage removed from beasts of burden, as some cruel writers of these days say; nor will I have you turn over with your foot the shabby horse-hair chairs that Leeby kept so speckless, and Hendry weaved for years to buy, and Jess so loved to look upon.

I speak of the chairs, but if we go together into the "room" they will not be visible to you. For a long time the house has been to let. Here, on the left of the doorway, as we enter, is the room, without a shred of furniture in it except the boards of two closed-in beds. The flooring is not steady, and here and there holes have been eaten into the planks. You can scarcely stand upright beneath the decaying ceiling. Worn boards and ragged walls, and the rusty ribs fallen from the fireplace, are all that meet your eyes, but I see a round, unsteady, waxcloth-covered table, with four books lying at equal distances on it. There are six prim chairs, two of them not to be sat upon, backed against the walls, and between the window and the fire-place a chest of drawers, with a snowy coverlet. On the drawers stands a board with coloured marbles for the game of solitaire, and I have only to open the drawer with the loose handle to bring out the dambrod. In the carved wood frame over the window hangs Jamie's portrait; in the only other frame a picture of Daniel in the den of lions, sewn by Leeby in wool. Over the chimney-piece with its shells, in which the roar of the sea can be heard, are strung three rows of birds' eggs. Once again we might be expecting company to tea.

The passage is narrow. There is a square hole between the rafters, and a ladder leading up to it. You may climb and look into the attic, as Jess liked to hear me call my tiny garret-room. I am stiffer now than in the days when I lodged with Jess during the summer holiday I am trying to bring back, and there is no need for me to ascend. Do not laugh at the newspapers with which Leeby papered the garret, nor at the yarn Hendry stuffed into the windy holes. He did it to warm the house for Jess. But the paper must have gone to pieces and the yarn rotted decades ago.

I have kept the kitchen for the last, as Jamie did on the dire day of which I shall have to tell. It has a flooring of stone now, where there used only to be hard earth, and a broken pane in the window is indifferently stuffed with rags. But it is the other window I turn to, with a pain at my heart, and pride and fondness too, the square foot of glass where Jess sat in her chair and looked down the brae.

Ah, that brae! The history of tragic little Thrums is sunk into it like the stones it swallows in the winter. We have all found the brae long and steep in the spring of life. Do you remember how the child you once were sat at the foot of it and wondered if a new world began at the top? It climbs from a shallow burn, and we used to sit on the brig a long time before venturing to climb. As boys we ran up the brae. As men and women, young and in our prime, we almost forgot that it was there. But the autumn of life comes, and the brae grows steeper; then the winter, and once again we are as the child pausing apprehensively on the brig. Yet are we no longer the child; we look now for no new world at the top, only for a little garden and a tiny house, and a handloom in the house. It is only a garden of kail and potatoes, but there may be a line of daisies, white and red, on each side of the narrow footpath, and honeysuckle over the door. Life is not always hard, even after backs grow bent, and we know that all braes lead only to the grave.

This is Jess's window. For more than twenty years she had not been able to go so far as the door, and only once while I knew her was she ben in the room. With her husband, Hendry, or their only daughter, Leeby, to lean upon, and her hand clutching her staff, she took twice a day, when she was strong, the journey between her bed and the window where stood her chair. She did not lie there looking at the sparrows or at Leeby redding up the house, and I hardly ever heard her complain. All the sewing was done by her; she often baked on a table pushed close to the window, and by leaning forward she could stir the porridge. Leeby was seldom off her feet, but I do not know that she did more than Jess, who liked to tell me, when she had a moment to spare, that she had a terrible lot to be thankful for.

To those who dwell in great cities Thrums is only a small place, but what a clatter of life it has for me when I come to it from my school-house in the glen. Had my lot been cast in a town I would no doubt have sought country parts during my September holiday, but the school-house is quiet even when the summer takes brakes full of sportsmen and others past the top of my footpath, and I was always light-hearted when Craigiebuckle's cart bore me into the din of Thrums. I only once stayed during the whole of my holiday at the house on the brae, but I knew its inmates for many years, including Jamie, the son, who was a barber in London. Of their ancestry I never heard. With us it was only some of the articles of furniture, or perhaps a snuff-mull, that had a genealogical tree. In the house on the brae was a great kettle, called the boiler, that was said to be fifty years old in the days of Hendry's grandfather, of whom nothing more is known. Jess's chair, which had carved arms and a seat stuffed with rags, had been Snecky Hobart's father's before it was hers, and old Snecky bought it at a roup in the Tenements. Jess's rarest possession was, perhaps, the christening robe that even people at a distance came to borrow. Her mother could count up a hundred persons who had been baptized in it.

Every one of the hundred, I believe, is dead, and even I cannot now pick out Jess and Hendry's grave; but I heard recently that the christening robe is still in use. It is strange that I should still be left after so many changes, one of the three or four who can to-day stand on the brae and point out Jess's window. The little window commands the incline to the point where the brae suddenly jerks out of sight in its climb down into the town. The steep path up the commonty makes for this elbow of the brae, and thus, whichever way the traveller takes, it is here that he comes first into sight of the window. Here, too, those who go to the town from the south get their first glimpse of Thrums.

Carts pass up and down the brae every few minutes, and there comes an occasional gig. Seldom is the brae empty, for many live beyond the top of it now, and men and women go by to their work, children to school or play. Not one of the children I see from the window to-day is known to me, and most of the men and women I only recognize by their likeness to their parents. That sweet-faced old woman with the shawl on her shoulders may be one of the girls who was playing at the game of palaulays when Jamie stole into Thrums for the last time; the man who is leaning on the commonty gate gathering breath for the last quarter of the brae may, as a barefooted callant, have been one of those who chased Cree Queery past the poor-house. I cannot say; but this I know, that the grandparents of most of these boys and girls were once young with me. If I see the sons and daughters of my friends grown old, I also see the grandchildren spinning the peerie and hunkering at I-dree-I-dree—I-droppit-it — as we did so long ago. The world remains as young as ever. The lovers that met on the commonty in the gloaming are gone, but there are other lovers to take their place, and still the commonty is here. The sun had sunk on a fine day in June, early in the century, when Hendry and Jess, newly married, he in a rich moleskin waistcoat, she in a white net cap, walked to the house on the brae that was to be their home. So Jess has told me. Here again has been just such a day, and somewhere in Thrums there may be just such a couple, setting out for their home behind a horse with white ears instead of walking, but with the same hopes and fears, and the same love light in their eyes. The world does not age. The hearse passes over the brae and up the straight burying-ground road, but still there is a cry for the christening robe.

Jess's window was a beacon by night to travellers in the dark, and it will be so in the future when there are none to remember Jess. There are many such windows still, with loving faces behind them. From them we watch for the friends and relatives who are coming back, and some alas! watch in vain. Not every one returns who takes the elbow of the brae bravely, or waves his handkerchief to those who watch from the window with wet eyes, and some return too late. To Jess, at her window always when she was not in bed, things happy and mournful and terrible came into view. At this window she sat for twenty years or more looking at the world as through a telescope; and here an awful ordeal was gone through after her sweet untarnished soul had been given back to God.

Chapter 2

ON THE TRACK OF THE MINISTER

On the afternoon of the Saturday that carted me and my two boxes to Thrums, I was ben in the room playing Hendry at the dambrod. I had one of the room chairs, but Leeby brought a chair from the kitchen for her father. Our door stood open, and as Hendry often pondered for two minutes with his hand on a "man," I could have joined in the gossip that was going on but the house.

"Ay, weel, then, Leeby," said Jess, suddenly, "I'll warrant the minister 'll no be preachin' the morn."

This took Leeby to the window.

"Yea, yea," she said (and I knew she was nodding her head sagaciously); I looked out at the room window, but all I could see was a man wheeling an empty barrow down the brae.

"That's Robbie Tosh," continued Leeby; "an' there's nae doot 'at he's makkin for the minister's, for he has on his black coat. He'll be to row the minister's luggage to the post-cart. Ay, an' that's Davit Lunan's barrow. I ken it by the shaft's bein' spliced wi' yarn. Davit broke the shaft at the saw-mill."

"He'll be gaen awa for a curran (number of) days," said Jess, "or he would juist hae taen his bag. Ay, he'll be awa to Edinbory, to see the lass."

"I wonder wha'll be to preach the morn—tod, it'll likely be Mr. Skinner, frae Dundee; him an' the minister's chief, ye ken."

"Ye micht gang up to the attic, Leeby, an' see if the spare bedroom vent (chimney) at the manse is gaen. We're sure, if it's Mr. Skinner, he'll come wi' the post frae Tilliedrum the nicht, an' sleep at the manse."

"Weel, I assure ye," said Leeby, descending from the attic, "it'll no be Mr. Skinner, for no only is the spare bedroom vent no gaen, but the blind's drawn doon frae tap to fut, so they're no even airin' the room. Na, it canna be him; an' what's mair, it'll be naebody 'at's to bide a' nicht at the manse."

"I wouldna say that; na, na. It may only be a student; an' Marget Dundas" (the minister's mother and housekeeper) "michtna think it necessary to put on a fire for him."

"Tod, I'll tell ye wha it'll be. I wonder I didna think o' 'im sooner. It'll be the lad Wilkie; him 'at's mither mairit on Sam'l Duthie's wife's brither. They bide in Cupar, an' I mind 'at when the son was here twa or three year syne he was juist gaen to begin the diveenity classes in Glesca."

"If that's so, Leeby, he would be sure to bide wi' Sam'l. Hendry, hae ye heard 'at Sam'l Duthie's expeckin' a stranger the nicht?"

"Haud yer tongue," replied Hendry, who was having the worst of the game.

"Ay, but I ken he is," said Leeby triumphantly to her mother, "for ye mind when I was in at Johnny Watt's (the draper's) Chirsty (Sam'l's wife) was buyin' twa yards o' chintz, an' I couldna think what she would be wantin' 't for!"

"I thocht Johnny said to ye 'at it was for a present to Chirsty's auntie?"

"Ay, but he juist guessed that; for, though he tried to get oot o' Chirsty what she wanted the chintz for, she wouldna tell 'im. But I see noo what she was after. The lad Wilkie 'll be to bide wi' them, and Chirsty had bocht the chintz to cover the arm-chair wi'. It's ane o' thae hair-bottomed chairs, but terrible torn, so she'll hae covered it for him to sit on."

"I wouldna wonder but ye're richt, Leeby; for Chirsty would be in an oncommon fluster if she thocht the lad's mither was likely to hear 'at her best chair was torn. Ay, ay, bein' a man, he wouldna think to tak aff the chintz an' hae a look at the chair withoot it."

Here Hendry, who had paid no attention to the conversation, broke in—

"Was ye speirin' had I seen Sam'l Duthie? I saw 'im yesterday buyin' a fender at Will'um Crook's roup."

"A fender! Ay, ay, that settles the queistion," said Leeby; "I'll warrant the fender was for Chirsty's parlour. It's preyed on Chirsty's mind, they say, this fower-and-thirty year 'at she doesna hae a richt parlour fender."

"Leeby, look! That's Robbie Tosh wi' the barrow. He has a michty load o' luggage. Am thinkin' the minister's bound for Tilliedrum."

"Na, he's no, he's gaen to Edinbory, as ye micht ken by the bandbox. That'll be his mither's bonnet he's takkin' back to get altered. Ye'll mind she was never pleased wi' the set o' the flowers."

"Weel, weel, here comes the minister himsel, an' very snod he is. Ay, Marget's been puttin' new braid on his coat, an' he's carryin' the sma' black bag he bocht in Dundee last year: he'll hae's nicht-shirt an' a comb in't, I dinna doot. Ye micht rin to' the corner, Leeby, an' see if he cries in at Jess McTaggart's in passin'."

"It's my opeenion," said Leeby, returning excitedly from the corner, " 'at the lad Wilkie's no to be preachin' the morn, after a'. When I gangs to the corner, at ony rate, what think ye's the first thing I see but the minister an' Sam'l Duthie meetin' face to face? Ay, weel, it's gospel am tellin' ye when I say as Sam'l flung back his head an' walkit richt by the minister!"

"Losh keep's a', Leeby; ye say that? They maun hae haen a quarrel."

"I'm thinkin' we'll hae Mr. Skinner i' the poopit the morn after a'."

"It may be, it may be. Ay, ay, look, Leeby, whatna bit kimmer's that wi' the twa jugs in her hand?"

"Eh? Ou, it'll be Lawyer Ogilvy's servant lassieky gaen to the farm o' T'nowhead for the milk. She gangs ilka Saturday nicht. But what did ye say — twa jugs? Tod, let's see! Ay, she has so, a big jug an' a little ane. The little ane 'll be for cream; an', sal, the big ane's bigger na usual."

"There maun be something gaen on at the lawyer's if they're buyin' cream, Leeby. Their reg'lar thing's twopence worth o' milk."

"Ay, but I assure ye that sma' jug's for cream, an' I dinna doot mysel but 'at there's to be fowerpence worth o' milk this nicht."

"There's to be a puddin' made the morn, Leeby. Ou, ay, a' thing points to that; an' we're very sure there's nae puddins at the lawyer's on the Sabbath onless they hae company."

"I dinna ken wha they can hae, if it be na that brither o' the wife's 'at bides oot by Aberdeen."

"Na, it's no him, Leeby; na, na. He's no weel to do, an' they wouldna be buyin' cream for 'im."

"I'll run up to the attic again, an' see if there's ony stir in the lawyer's hoose."

By and by Leeby returned in triumph.

"Ou, ay," she said, "they're expectin' veesitors at the lawyer's, for I could see twa o' the bairns dressed up to the nines, an' Mistress Ogilvy doesnae dress at them in that wy for naething."

"It fair beats me though, Leeby, to guess wha's comin' to them. Ay, but stop a meenute, I wouldnae wonder, no, really I would not wonder but what it'll be — "

"The very thing 'at was passin' through my head, mother."

"Ye mean 'at the lad Wilkie 'll be to bide wi' the lawyer i'stead o' wi' Sam'l Duthie? Sal, am thinkin' that's it. Ye ken Sam'l an' the lawyer married on cousins; but Mistress Ogilvy aye lookit on Chirsty as dirt aneath her feet. She would be glad to get a minister, though, to the hoose, an' so I warrant the lad Wilkie 'll be to bide a' nicht at the lawyer's."

"But what would Chirsty be doin' gettin' the chintz an' the fender in that case?"

"Ou, she'd been expeckin' the lad, of course. Sal, she'll be in a michty tantrum aboot this. I wouldna wonder though she gets Sam'l to gang ower to the U.P.'s."

Leeby went once more to the attic.

"Ye're wrang, mother," she cried out. "Whaever's to preach the morn is to bide at the manse, for the minister's servant's been at Baker Duff's buyin' short-bread—half a lippy, nae doot."

"Are ye sure o' that, Leeby ?"

"Oh, am certain. The servant gaed in to Duffs the noo, an', as ye ken fine, the manse fowk doesna deal wi' him, except they're wantin' short-bread. He's Auld Kirk."

Leeby returned to the kitchen, and Jess sat for a time ruminating.

"The lad Wilkie," she said at last, triumphantly, " 'll be to bide at Lawyer Ogilvy's; but he'll be gaen to the manse the morn for a tea-dinner."

"But what," asked Leeby, "aboot the milk an' the cream for the lawyer's?"

"Ou, they'll be hae'n a puddin' for the supper the nicht. That's a michty genteel thing, I've heard."

It turned out that Jess was right in every particular.

Chapter 3

PREPARING TO RECEIVE COMPANY

Leeby was at the fire brandering a quarter of steak on the tongs, when the house was flung into consternation by Hendry's casual remark that he had seen Tibbie Mealmaker in the town with her man.

"The Lord preserve's!" cried Leeby.

Jess looked quickly at the clock.

"Half fower!" she said excitedly.

"Then it canna be dune" said Leeby, falling despairingly into a chair, "for they may be here ony meenute."

"It's, most michty," said Jess, turning on her husband, " 'at ye should tak a pleasure in bringin' this hoose to disgrace. Hoo did ye no tell's suner?"

"I fair forgot," Hendry answered, "but what's a' yer steer?"

Jess looked at me (she often did this) in a way that meant, "What a man is this I'm tied to!"

"Steer!" she exclaimed. "Is't no time we was makkin' a steer? They'll be in for their tea ony meenute, an' the room no sae muckle as sweepit. Ay, an' me lookin' like a sweep; an' Tibbie Mealmaker 'at's sae partikler genteel seein' you sic a sicht as ye are!"

Jess shook Hendry out of his chair, while Leeby began to sweep with the one hand, and agitatedly to unbutton her wrapper with the other.

"She didna see me," said Hendry, sitting down forlornly on the table.

"Get aff that table!" cried Jess. "See haud o' the besom," she said to Leeby.

"For mercy's sake, mother," said Leeby, "gie yer face a dicht, an' put on a clean mutch."

"I'll open the door if they come afore you're ready," said Hendry, as Leeby pushed him against the dresser.

"Ye daur to speak aboot openin' the door, an' you sic a mess!" cried Jess, with pins in her mouth.

"Havers!" retorted Hendry. A man canna be aye washin' at 'imsel."

Seeing that Hendry was as much in the way as myself, I invited him upstairs to the attic, whence we heard Jess and Leeby upbraiding each other shrilly. I was aware that the room was speckless; but for all that, Leeby was turning it upside down.

"She's aye ta'en like that," Hendry said to me, referring to his wife, "when she's expectin' company. Ay, it's a peety she canna tak things cannier."

"Tibbie Mealmaker must be some one of importance?" I asked.

"Ou, she's naething by the ord'nar'; but ye see she was mairit to a Tilliedrum man no lang syne, an' they're said to hae a michty grand establishment. Ay, they've a wardrobe spleet new; an' what think ye Tibbie wears ilka day?"

I shook my head.

"It was Chirsty Miller 'at put it through the toon," Hendry continued. "Chirsty was in Tilliedrum last Teisday or Wednesday, an' Tibbie gae her a cup o' tea. Ay, weel, Tibbie telt Chirsty 'at she wears hose ilka day."

"Wears hose?"

"Ay. It's some michty grand kind o' stockin'. I never heard o't in this toon. Na, there's naebody in Thrums 'at wears hose."

"And who did Tibbie get?" I asked; for in Thrums they say, "Wha did she get?" and "Wha did he tak?"

"His name's Davit Curly. Ou, a crittur fu' o' maggots, an' nae great match, for he's juist the Tilliedrum bill-sticker."

At this moment Jess shouted from her chair (she was burnishing the society teapot as she spoke), "Mind Hendry McQumpha, 'at upon nae condition are ye to mention the bill-stickin' afore Tibbie!"

"Tibbie," Hendry explained to me, "is a terrible vain tid, an' doesna think the bill-stickin' genteel. Ay, they say 'at if she meets Davit in the street wi' his paste-pot an' the brush in his hands she pretends no to ken 'im."

Every time Jess paused to think she cried up orders, such as—

"Dinna call her Tibbie, mind ye. Always address her as Mistress Curly."

"Shak' hands wi'baith o' them, an' say ye hope they're in the enjoyment o' guid health."

"Dinna put yer feet on the table."

"Mind, you're no' to mention 'at ye kent they were in the toon."

"When onybody passes ye yer tea say, 'Thank ye.'"

"Dinna stir yer tea as if ye was churnin' butter, nor let on 'at the scones is no our ain bakin'."

"If Tibbie says onything aboot the china yer no' to say 'at we dinna use it ilka day."

"Dinna lean back in the big chair, for it's broken, an' Leeby's gi'en it a lick o' glue this meenute."

"When Leeby gies ye a kick aneath the table that'll be a sign to ye to say grace."

Hendry looked at me apologetically while these instructions came up.

"I winna dive my head wi' sic nonsense," he said; "it's no' for a man body to be sae crammed fu' o' manners."

"Come awa doon," Jess shouted to him, "an' put on a clean dickey."

"I'll better do't to please her," said Hendry, "though for my ain part I dinna like the feel o' a dickey on week-days. Na, they mak's think it's the Sabbath."

Ten minutes afterwards I went downstairs to see how the preparations were progressing. Fresh muslin curtains had been put up in the room. The grand footstool, worked by Leeby, was so placed that Tibbie could not help seeing it; and a fine cambric handkerchief, of which Jess was very proud, was hanging out of a drawer as if by accident. An antimacassar lying carelessly on the seat of a chair concealed a rent in the horse-hair, and the china ornaments on the mantelpiece were so placed that they looked whole. Leeby's black merino was hanging near the window in a good light, and Jess's Sabbath bonnet, which was never worn, occupied a nail beside it. The tea-things stood on a tray in the kitchen bed, whence they could be quickly brought into the room, just as if they were always ready to be used daily. Leeby, as yet in deshabille, was shaving her father at a tremendous rate, and Jess, looking as fresh as a daisy, was ready to receive the visitors. She was peering through the tiny window-blind looking for them.

"Be cautious, Leeby," Hendry was saying, when Jess shook her hand at him. "Wheesht," she whispered ; "they're comin'."

Hendry was hustled into his Sabbath coat, and then came a tap at the door, a very genteel tap. Jess nodded to Leeby, who softly shoved Hendry into the room.

The tap was repeated, but Leeby pushed her father into a chair and thrust Barrow's Sermons open into his hand. Then she stole but the house, and swiftly buttoned her wrapper, speaking to Jess by nods the while. There was a third knock, whereupon Jess said, in a loud, Englishy voice

"Was not that a chap (knock) at the door?"

Hendry was about to reply, but she shook her fist at him. Next moment Leeby opened the door. I was upstairs, but I heard Jess say—

"Dear me, if it's not Mrs. Curly — and Mr. Curly! And hoo are ye? Come in, by. Weel, this is, indeed, a pleasant surprise!"

Chapter 4

WAITING FOR THE DOCTOR

Jess had gone early to rest, and the door of her bed in the kitchen was pulled to. From her window I saw Hendry buying dulse.

Now and again the dulseman wheeled his slimy boxes to the top of the brae, and sat there stolidly on the shafts of his barrow. Many passed him by, but occasionally some one came to rest by his side. Unless the customer was loquacious, there was no bandying of words, and Hendry merely unbuttoned his east-trouser pocket, giving his body the angle at which the pocket could be most easily filled by the dulseman. He then deposited his halfpenny, and moved on. Neither had spoken; yet in the country they would have roared their predictions about to-morrow to a ploughman half a field away.

Dulse is roasted by twisting it round the tongs fired to a red-heat, and the house was soon heavy with the smell of burning sea-weed. Leeby was at the dresser munching it from a broth-plate, while Hendry, on his knees at the fireplace, gingerly tore off the blades of dulse that were sticking to the tongs, and licked his singed fingers.

"Whaur's yer mother?" he asked Leeby.

"Ou," said Leeby, " whaur would she be but in her bed?"

Hendry took the tongs to the door, and would have cleaned them himself, had not Leeby (who often talked his interfering ways over with her mother) torn them from his hands.

"Leeby!" cried Jess at that moment.

"Ay," answered Leeby, leisurely, not noticing, as I happened to do, that Jess spoke in an agitated voice.

"What is't? " asked Hendry, who liked to be told things.

He opened the door of the bed.

"Yer mother's no weel," he said to Leeby.

Leeby ran to the bed, and I went ben the house.

In another two minutes we were a group of four in the kitchen, staring vacantly. Death could not have startled us more, tapping thrice that quiet night on the window-pane.

"It's diphtheria!" said Jess, her hands trembling as she buttoned her wrapper.

She looked at me, and Leeby looked at me.

"It's no, it's no," cried Leeby, and her voice was as a fist shaken at my face. She blamed me for hesitating in my reply. But ever since this malady left me a lonely dominie for life, diphtheria has been a knockdown word for me. Jess had discovered a great white spot on her throat. I knew the symptoms.

"Is't dangerous?" asked Hendry, who once had a headache years before, and could still refer to it as a reminiscence.

"Them 'at has 't never recovers," said Jess, sitting down very quietly. A stick fell from the fire, and she bent forward to replace it.

"They do recover," cried Leeby, again turning angry eyes on me.

I could not face her; I had known so many who did not recover. She put her hand on her mother's shoulder.

"Mebbe you would be better in yer bed," suggested Hendry.

No one spoke.

"When I had the headache," said Hendry, "I was better in my bed."

Leeby had taken Jess's hand — a worn old hand that had many a time gone out in love and kindness when younger hands were cold. Poets have sung and fighting men have done great deeds for hands that never had such a record.

"If ye could eat something," said Hendry, "I would gae to the flesher's for 't. I mind when I had the headache, hoo a small steak—— "

"Gae awa for the doctor, rayther," broke in Leeby.

Jess started, for sufferers think there is less hope for them after the doctor has been called in to pronounce sentence.

"I winna hae the doctor," she said, anxiously.

In answer to Leeby's nods, Hendry slowly pulled out his boots from beneath the table, and sat looking at them, preparatory to putting them on. He was beginning at last to be a little scared, though his face did not show it.

"I winna hae ye," cried Jess, getting to her feet, "ga'en to the doctor's sic a sicht. Yer coat's a' yarn."

"Havers," said Hendry, but Jess became frantic.

I offered to go for the doctor, but while I was upstairs looking for my bonnet I heard the door slam. Leeby had become impatient, and darted off herself, buttoning her jacket probably as she ran. When I returned to the kitchen, Jess and Hendry were still by the fire. Hendry was beating a charred stick into sparks, and his wife sat with her hands in her lap. I saw Hendry look at her once or twice, but he could think of nothing to say. His terms of endearment had died out thirty-nine years before with his courtship. He had forgotten the words. For his life he could not have crossed over to Jess and put his arm round her. Yet he was uneasy. His eyes wandered round the poorly lit room.

"Will ye hae a drink o' watter?" he asked.

There was a sound of footsteps outside.

"That'll be him," said Hendry in a whisper.

Jess started to her feet, and told Hendry to help her ben the house.

The steps died away, but I fancied that Jess, now highly strung, had gone into hiding, and I went after her. I was mistaken. She had lit the room lamp, turning the crack in the globe to the wall. The sheepskin hearthrug, which was generally carefully packed away beneath the bed, had been spread out before the empty fireplace, and Jess was on the arm-chair hurriedly putting on her grand black mutch with the pink flowers.

"I was juist makkin' mysel respectable," she said, but without life in her voice.

This was the only time I ever saw her in the room.

Leeby returned panting to say that the doctor might be expected in an hour. He was away among the hills.

The hour passed reluctantly. Leeby lit a fire ben the house, and then put on her Sabbath dress. She sat with her mother in the room. Never before had I seen Jess sit so quietly, for her way was to work until, as she said herself, she was ready "to fall into her bed."

Hendry wandered between the two rooms, always in the way when Leeby ran to the window to see if that was the doctor at last. He would stand gaping in the middle of the room for five minutes, then slowly withdraw to stand as drearily but the house. His face lengthened. At last he sat down by the kitchen fire, a Bible in his hand. It lay open on his knee, but he did not read much. He sat there with his legs outstretched, looking straight before him. I believe he saw Jess young again. His face was very solemn, and his mouth twitched. The fire sank into ashes unheeded.

I sat alone at my attic window for hours, waiting for the doctor. From the attic I could see nearly all Thrums, but, until very late, the night was dark, and the brae, except immediately before the door, was blurred and dim. A sheet of light canopied the square as long as a cheap Jack paraded his goods there. It was gone before the moon came out. Figures tramped, tramped up the brae, passed the house in shadow and stole silently on. A man or boy whistling seemed to fill the valley. The moon arrived too late to be of service to any wayfarer. Everybody in Thrums was asleep but ourselves, and the doctor who never came.

About midnight Hendry climbed the attic stair and joined me at the window. His hand was shaking as he pulled back the blind. I began to realize that his heart could still overflow.

"She's waur," he whispered, like one who had lost his voice.

For a long time he sat silently, his hand on the blind. He was so different from the Hendry I had known, that I felt myself in the presence of a strange man. His eyes were glazed with staring at the turn of the brae where the doctor must first come into sight. His breathing became heavier, till it was a gasp. Then I put my hand on his shoulder, and he stared at me.

"Nine-and-thirty years come June," he said, speaking to himself.

For this length of time, I knew, he and Jess had been married. He repeated the words at intervals. "I mind"— he began, and stopped. He was thinking of the spring-time of Jess's life.

The night ended as we watched; then came the terrible moment that precedes the day—the moment known to shuddering watchers by sick beds, when a chill wind cuts through the house, and the world without seems cold in death. It is as if the heart of the earth did not mean to continue beating.

"This is a fearsome nicht," Hendry said, hoarsely.

He turned to grope his way to the stairs, but suddenly went down on his knees to pray. . . .

There was a quick step outside. I arose in time to see the doctor on the brae. He tried the latch, but Leeby was there to show him in. The door of the room closed on him.

From the top of the stair I could see into the dark passage, and make out Hendry shaking at the door. I could hear the doctor's voice, but not the words he said. There was a painful silence, and then Leeby laughed joyously.

"It's gone," cried Jess; "the white spot's gone! Ye juist touched it, an' it's gone! Tell Hendry."

But Hendry did not need to be told. As Jess spoke I heard him say, huskily: "Thank God!" and then he tottered back to the kitchen. When the doctor left, Hendry was still on Jess's arm-chair, trembling like a man with the palsy. Ten minutes afterwards I was preparing for bed, when he cried up the stair—

"Come awa' doon."

I joined the family party in the room: Hendry was sitting close to Jess.

"Let us read," he said, firmly, "in the fourteenth of John."

Chapter 5

A HUMORIST ON HIS CALLING

After the eight o'clock bell had rung, Hendry occasionally crossed over to the farm of T'nowhead and sat on the pig-sty. If no one joined him he scratched the pig, and returned home gradually. Here what was almost a club held informal meetings, at which two or four, or even half a dozen assembled to debate, when there was any one to start them. The meetings were only memorable when Tammas Haggart was in fettle, to pronounce judgments in his well-known sarcastic way. Sometimes we had got off the pig-sty to separate before Tammas was properly yoked. There we might remain a long time, planted round him like trees, for he was a mesmerising talker.

There was a pail belonging to the pig-sty which some one would turn bottom upwards and sit upon if the attendance was unusually numerous. Tammas liked, however, to put a foot on it now and again in the full swing of a harangue, and when he paused for a sarcasm I have seen the pail kicked toward him. He had the wave of the arm that is so convincing in argument, and such a natural way of asking questions, that an audience not used to public speaking might have thought he wanted them to reply. It is an undoubted fact, that when he went on the platform, at the time of the election, to heckle the Colonel, he paused in the middle of his questions to take a drink out of the tumbler of water which stood on the table. As soon as they saw what he was up to, the spectators raised a ringing cheer.

On concluding his perorations, Tammas sent his snuff-mull round, but we had our own way of passing him a vote of thanks. One of the company would express amazement at his gift of words, and the others would add, "Man, man," or, "Ye cow, Tammas," or,

"What a crittur ye are!" all which ejaculations meant the same thing. A new subject being thus ingeniously introduced, Tammas again put his foot on the pail.

"I tak no creedit," he said modestly, on the evening, I remember, of Willie Pyatt's funeral, "in bein' able to speak wi' a sort o' faceelity on topics 'at I've made my ain."

"Ay," said T'nowhead, "but it's no the faceelity o' speakin' 'at taks me. There's Davit Lunan 'at can speak like as if he had learned it aff a paper, an' yet I canna thole 'im."

"Davit," said Hendry, "doesna speak in a wy 'at a body can follow 'im. He doesna gae even on. Jess says he's juist like a man aye at the cross-roads, an' no sure o' his wy. But the stock has words, an' no ilka body has that."

"If I was bidden to put Tammas's gift in a word," said T'nowhead, "I would say 'at he had a wy. That's what I would say."

"Weel, I suppose I have," Tammas admitted, "but wy or no wy, I couldna put a point on my words if it wasna for my sense o' humour. Lads, humour's what gies the nip to speakin'."

"It's what maks ye a sarcesticist, Tammas," said Hendry; "but what I wonder at is yer sayin' the humorous things sae aisy like. Some says ye mak them up aforehand, but I ken that's no true."

"No only is't no true," said Tammas, "but it couldna be true. Them 'at says sic things, an', weel I ken you're meanin' Davit Lunan, hasna nae idea o' what humour is. It's a thing 'at spouts oot o' its ain accord. Some o' the maist humorous things I've ever said cam oot, as a body may say, by themsels."

"I suppose that's the case," said T'nowhead, "an' yet it maun be you 'at brings them up?"

"There's no nae doubt aboot its bein' the case," said Tammas, "for I've watched mysel often. There was a vara guid instance occurred sune after I married Easie. The Earl's son met me one day, aboot that time, i' the Tenements, an' he didna ken 'at Chirsty was deid, an' I'd married again. 'Well, Haggart,' he says, in his frank wy, 'and how is your wife?' 'She's vara weel, sir,' I maks answer, 'but she's no the ane you mean.' "

"Na, he meant Chirsty," said Hendry.

"Is that a' the story?" asked T'nowhead.

Tammas had been looking at us queerly.

"There's no nane o' ye lauchin'," he said, but I can assure ye the Earl's son gaed east the toon lauchin' like onything."

"But what was't he lauched at?"

"Ou," said Tammas, "a humorist doesna tell whaur the humour comes in."

"No, but when you said that, did ye mean it to be humorous?"

"Am no sayin' I did, but as I've been tellin' ye humour spouts oot by itsel."

"Ay, but do ye ken noo what the Earl's son gaed awa lauchin' at?"

Tammas hesitated.

"I dinna exactly see't," he confessed, "but that's no an oncommon thing. A humorist would often no ken 'at he was ane if it wasna by the wy he maks other fowk lauch. A body canna be expeckit baith to mak the joke an' to see't. Na, that would be doin' twa fowks' wark."

"Weel, that's reasonable enough, but I've often seen ye lauchin'," said Hendry, "lang afore other fowk lauched."

"Nae doubt," Tammas explained, "an' that's because humour has twa sides, juist like a penny piece. When I say a humorous thing mysel, I'm dependent on other fowk to tak note o' the humour o't, bein' mysel ta'en up wi' the makkin' o't. Ay, but there's things I see an' hear 'at maks me lauch, an' that's the other side o' humour."

"I never heard it put sae plain afore," said T'nowhead, "an', sal, am no nane sure but what am a humorist too."

" Na, na, no you, T'nowhead," said Tammas, hotly.

"Weel," continued the farmer, "I never set up for bein' a humorist, but I can juist assure ye 'at I lauch at queer things too. No lang syne I woke up i' my bed lauchin' like onything, an' Lisbeth thocht I wasna weel. It was something I dreamed 'at made me lauch, I couldna think what it was, but I lauched richt. Was that no fell like a humorist?"

"That was neither here nor there," said Tammas. "Na, dreams dinna coont, for we're no responsible for them. Ay, an' what's mair, the mere lauchin's no the important side o' humour, even though ye hinna to be telt to lauch. The important side's the other side, the sayin' the humorous things I'll tell ye what: the humorist's like a man firin' at a target he doesna ken whether he hits or no till them at the target tells 'im."

"I would be of opeenion," said Hendry, who was one of Tammas's most staunch admirers, " 'at another mark o' the rale humorist was his seein' humour in all things?"

Tammas shook his head — a way he had when Hendry advanced theories.

"I dinna haud wi' that ava," he said. " I ken fine 'at Davit Lunan gaes aboot sayin' he sees humour in everything, but there's nae surer sign at he's no a genuine humorist. Na, the rale humorist kens vara weel 'at there's subjects withoot a spark o'humour in them. When a subject rises to the sublime it should be regarded philosophically, an' no humorously. Davit would lauch 'at the grandest thochts, whaur they only fill the true humorist wi' awe. I've found it necessary to rebuke 'im at times whaur his lauchin' was oot o' place. He pretended aince on this vara spot to see humour i' the origin o' cock-fightin'."

"Did he, man?" said Hendry; "I wasna here. But what is the origin o' cock-fechtin'?"

"It was a' i' the *Cheap Magazine*," said T'nowhead.

"Was I sayin' it wasna?" demanded Tammas. "It was through me readin' the account oot o' the *Cheap Magazine* 'at the discussion arose."

"But what said the *Cheapy* was the origin o' cock-fechtin'?"

"T'nowhead 'll tell ye," answered Tammas; "he says I dinna ken."

"I never said naething o' the kind," returned T'nowhead, indignantly; "I mind o' ye readin't oot fine."

"Ay, weel," said Tammas, "that's a' richt. Ou, the origin o' cock-fightin' gangs back to the time o' the Greek wars, a thoosand or twa years syne, mair or less. There was ane, Miltiades by name, 'at was the captain o' the Greek army, an' one day he led them doon the mountains to attack the biggest army 'at was ever gathered thegither."

"They were Persians," interposed T'nowhead.

"Are you tellin' the story, or am I?" asked Tammas. "I kent fine 'at they were Persians. Weel, Miltiades had the matter o' twenty thoosand men wi' 'im, and when they got to the foot o' the mountain, behold there was two cocks fechtin'."

"Man, man," said Hendry, "an' was there cocks in thae days?"

"Ondoubtedly," said Tammas, "or hoo could thae twa hae been fechtin'?"

"Ye have me there, Tammas," admitted Hendry. "Ye're perfectly richt."

"Ay, then," continued the stone-breaker, "when Miltiades saw the cocks at it wi' all their micht, he stepped the army and addressed it. 'Behold!' he cried, at the top o' his voice, 'these cocks do not fight for their household gods, nor for the monuments of their ancestors, nor for glory, nor for liberty, nor for their children, but only because the one will not give way unto the other.'"

"It was nobly said," declared Hendry; "na, cocks wouldna hae sae muckle understandin' as to fecht for thae things. I wouldna wonder but what it was some laddies 'at set them at ane another."

"Hendry doesna see what Miltydes was after," said T'nowhead.

"Ye've taen't up wrang, Hendry," Tammas explained. "What Miltiades meant was 'at if cocks could fecht sae weel oot o' mere deviltry, surely the Greeks would fecht terrible for their gods an' their bairns an' the other things."

"I see, I see; but what was the monuments o' their ancestors?"

"Ou, that was the gravestanes they put up i' their kirkyards."

"I wonder the other billies would want to tak them awa. They would be a michty wecht."

"Ay, but they wanted them, an' nat'rally the Greeks stuck to the stanes they paid for."

"So, so, an' did Davit Lunan mak oot 'at there was humour in that?"

"He do so. He said it was a humorous thing to think o' a hale army lookin' on at twa cocks fechtin'. I assure ye I telt 'im 'at I saw nae humour in't. It was ane o' the most impressive sichts ever seen by man, an' the Greeks was sae inspired by what Miltiades said 'at they sweepit the Persians oot o' their country."

We all agreed that Tammas's was the genuine humour.

"An' an enviable possession it is," said Hendry.

"In a wy," admitted Tammas, "but no in a' wys."

He hesitated, and then added in a low voice —

"As sure as death, Hendry, it sometimes taks grip o' me i' the kirk itsel, an' I can hardly keep frae lauchin'."

Chapter 6

DEAD THIS TWENTY YEARS

In the lustiness of youth there are many who cannot feel that they, too, will die. The first fear stops the heart. Even then they would keep death at arm's length by making believe to disown him. Loved ones are taken away, and the boy, the girl, will not speak of them, as if that made the conqueror's triumph the less. In time the fire in the breast burns low, and then in the last glow of the embers, it is sweeter to hold to what has been than to think of what may be.

Twenty years had passed since Joey ran down the brae to play. Jess, his mother, shook her staff fondly at him. A cart rumbled by, the driver nodding on the shaft. It rounded the corner and stopped suddenly, and then a woman screamed. A handful of men carried Joey's dead body to his mother, and that was the tragedy of Jess's life.

Twenty years ago, and still Jess sat at the window, and still she heard that woman scream. Every other living being had forgotten Joey; even to Hendry he was now scarcely a name, but there were times when Jess's face quivered and her old arms went out for her dead boy.

"God's will be done," she said, "but oh, I grudged Him my bairn terrible sair. I dinna want him back noo, an' ilka day is takkin' me nearer to him, but for mony a lang year I grudged him sair, sair. He was juist five minutes gone, an' they brocht him back deid, my Joey."

On the Sabbath day Jess could not go to church, and it was then, I think, that she was with Joey most. There was often a blessed serenity on her face when we returned, that only comes to those who have risen from their knees with their prayers answered. Then she was very close to the boy who died. Long ago she could not look out from her window upon the brae, but now it was her seat in church. There on the Sabbath evenings she sometimes talked to me of Joey.

"It's been a fine day," she would say, "juist like that day. I thank the Lord for the sunshine noo, but oh, I thocht at the time I couldna look at the sun shinin' again."

"In all Thrums," she has told me, and I know it to be true, "there's no a better man than Hendry. There's them 'at's cleverer in the wys o' the world, but my man, Hendry McQumpha, never did naething in all his life 'at wasna weel intended, an' though his words is common, it's to the Lord he looks. I canna think but what Hendry's pleasin' to God. Oh, I dinna ken what to say wi' thankfulness to Him when I mind hoo guid He's been to me. There's Leeby 'at I couldna hae done withoot, me bein' sae silly (weak bodily), an' ay Leeby's stuck by me an' gien up her life, as ye micht say, for me. Jamie — "

But then Jess sometimes broke down.

"He's so far awa," she said, after a time, "an' aye when he gangs back to London after his holidays he has a fear he'll never see me again, but he's terrified to mention it, an' I juist ken by the wy he taks haud o' me, an' comes runnin' back to tak haud o' me again. I ken fine what he's thinkin', but I daurna speak.

"Guid is no word for what Jamie has been to me, but he wasna born till after Joey died. When we got Jamie, Hendry took to whistlin' again at the loom, an' Jamie juist filled Joey's place to him. Ay, but naebody could fill Joey's place to me. It's different to a man. A bairn's no the same to him, but a fell bit o' me was buried in my laddie's grave.

"Jamie an' Joey was never nane the same nature. It was aye something in a shop, Jamie wanted to be, an' he never cared muckle for his books, but Joey hankered after being a minister, young as he was, an' a minister Hendry an' me would hae done our best to mak him. Mony, mony a time after he came in frae the kirk on the Sabbath he would stand up at this very window and wave his hands in a reverent way, juist like the minister. His first text was to be 'Thou God seest me.'

"Ye'll wonder at me, but I've sat here in the lang fore-nichts dreamin' 'at Joey was a grown man noo, an' 'at I was puttin' on my bonnet to come to the kirk to hear him preach. Even as far back as twenty years an' mair I wasna able to gang aboot, but Joey would say to me, 'We'll get a carriage to ye, mother, so 'at ye can come and hear me preach on "Thou God seest me." ' He would say to me, 'It doesna do, mother, for the minister in the pulpit to nod to ony o' the fowk, but I'll gie ye a look an' ye'll ken it's me.' Oh, Joey, I would hae gien you a look too, an' ye would hae kent what I was thinkin'. He often said, 'Ye'll be proud o' me, will ye no, mother, when ye see me comin' sailin' alang to the pulpit in my gown?' So I would hae been proud o' him, an' I was proud to hear him speakin' o't. 'The other fowk,' he said, 'will be sittin' in their seats wonderin' what my text's to be, but you'll ken, mother, an' you'll turn up to "Thou God seest me," afore I gie oot the chapter.' Ay, but that day he was coffined, for all the minister prayed, I found it hard to say, 'Thou God seest me.' It's the text I like best noo, though, an' when Hendry an' Leeby is at the kirk, I turn't up often, often in the Bible. I read frae the beginnin' o' the chapter, but when I come to 'Thou God seest me,' I stop. Na, it's no 'at there's ony rebellion to the Lord in my heart noo, for I ken He was lookin' doon when the cart gaed ower Joey, an' He wanted to tak my laddie to Himsel. But juist when I come to 'Thou God seest me,' I let the Book lie in my lap, for aince a body's sure o' that they're sure o' all. Ay, ye'll laugh, but I think, mebbe juist because I was his mother, 'at though Joey never lived to preach in a kirk, he's preached frae 'Thou God seest me' to me. I dinna ken 'at I would ever hae been sae sure o' that if it hadna been for him, an' so I think I see 'im sailin' doon to the pulpit juist as he said he would do. I seen him gien me the look he spoke o' — ay, he looks my wy first, an' I ken it's him. Naebody sees him but me, but I see him gien me the look he promised. He's so terrible near me, an' him dead, 'at when my time comes I'll be rale willin' to go. I dinna say that to Jamie, because he all trembles; but I'm auld noo, an' I'm no nane loth to gang."

Jess's staff probably had a history before it became hers, for, as known to me it was always old and black. If we studied them sufficiently we might discover that staves age perceptibly just as the hair turns grey. At the risk of being thought fanciful I dare to say that in inanimate objects, as in ourselves, there is honourable and shameful old age, and that to me Jess's staff was a symbol of the good, the true. It rested against her in the window, and she was so helpless without it when on her feet, that to those who saw much of her it was part of herself. The staff was very short, nearly a foot having been cut, as I think she once told me herself, from the original, of which to make a porridge thieval (or stick with which to stir porridge), and in moving Jess leant heavily on it. Had she stood erect it would not have touched the floor. This was the staff that Jess shook so joyfully at her boy the forenoon in May when he ran out to his death. Joey, however, was associated in Jess's memory with her staff in less painful ways. When she spoke of him she took the dwarf of a staff in her hands and looked at it softly.

"It's hard to me," she would say, "to believe 'at twa an' twenty years hae come and gone since the nicht Joey hod (hid) my staff. Ay, but Hendry was straucht in thae days by what he is noo, an' Jamie wasna born. Twa an' twenty years come the back end o' the year, an' it wasna thocht 'at I could live through the winter. 'Ye'll no last mair than anither month, Jess,' was what my sister Bell said, when she came to see me, and yet here I am aye sittin' at my window, an' Bell's been i' the kirkyard this dozen years.

"Leeby was saxteen month younger than Joey, an' mair quiet like. Her heart was juist set on helpin' aboot the hoose, an' though she was but fower year auld she could kindle the fire an' red up (clean up) the room. Leeby's been my savin' ever since she was fower year auld. Ay, but it was Joey 'at hung aboot me maist, an' he took notice 'at I wasna gaen out as I used to do. Since sune after my marriage I've needed the stick, but there was days 'at I could gang across the road an' sit on a stane. Joey kent there was something wrang when I had to gie that up, an' syne he noticed 'at

I couldna even gang to the window unless Hendry kind o' carried me. Na, ye wouldna think 'at there could hae been days when Hendry did that, but he did. He was a sort o' ashamed if ony o' the neighbours saw him so affectionate like, but he was terrible taen up aboot me. His loom was doon at T'nowhead's Bell's father's, an' often he cam awa up to see if I was ony better. He didna lat on to the other weavers 'at he was comin' to see what like I was. Na, he juist said he'd forgotten a pirn, or his cruizey lamp, or onything. Ah, but he didna mak nae pretence o' no carin' for me aince he was inside the hoose. He came crawlin' to the bed no to wauken me if I was sleepin', an' mony a time I made belief 'at I was, juist to please him. It was an awfu' business on him to hae a young wife sae helpless, but he wasna the man to cast that at me. I mind o' sayin' to him one day in my bed, 'Ye made a poor bargain, Hendry, when ye took me.' But he says, 'Not one soul in Thrums'll daur say that to me but yersel, Jess. Na, na, my dawty, you're the wuman o' my choice; there's juist one wuman i' the warld to me, an' that's you, my ain Jess.' Twa an' twenty years syne. Ay, Hendry called me fond like names, thae no everyday names. What a straucht man he was!

"The doctor had said he could do no more for me, an' Hendry was the only ane 'at didna gie me up. The bairns, of course, didna understan', and Joey would come into the bed an' play on the top o' me. Hendry would hae ta'en him awa, but I liked to hae 'im. Ye see, we was lang married afore we had a bairn, an' though I couldna bear ony other weight on me, Joey didna hurt me, somehoo. I liked to hae 'im so close to me.

"It was through that 'at he came to bury my staff. I couldna help often thinkin' o' what like the hoose would be when I was gone, an' aboot Leeby an' Joey left so young. So, when I could say it without greetin', I said to Joey 'at I was goin' far awa, an' would he be a terrible guid laddie to his father and Leeby when I was gone? He aye juist said, 'Dinna gang, mother, dinna gang,' but one day Hendry came in frae his loom, and says Joey, 'Father, whaur's my mother gaen to, awa frae us?' I'll never forget Hendry's face. His mooth juist opened an' shut twa or three times, an' he walked quick ben to the room. I cried oot to him to come back, but he didna come, so I sent Joey for him. Joey came runnin' back to me sayin', 'Mother, mother, am awfu' fleid (frightened), for my father's greetin' sair.'

"A' thae things took a haud o' Joey, an' he ended in gien us a fleg (fright). I was sleepin' ill at the time, an' Hendry was ben sleepin' in the room wi' Leeby, Joey bein' wi' me. Ay, weel, one nicht I woke up in the dark an' put oot my hand to 'im, an' he wasna there. I sat up wi' a terrible start, an' syne I kent by the cauld 'at the door maun be open. I cried oot quick to Hendry, but he was a soond sleeper, an' he didna hear me. Ay, I dinna ken hoo I did it, but I got ben to the room an' shook him up. I was near daft wi' fear when I saw Leeby wasna there either. Hendry couldna tak it in a' at aince, but sune he had his trousers on, an' he made me lie down on his bed. He said he wouldna move till I did it, or I wouldna hae dune it. As sune as he was oot o' the hoose crying their names I sat up in my bed listenin'. Sune I heard speakin', an' in a minute Leeby comes runnin' in to me, roarin' an' greetin'. She was barefeeted, and had juist her nichtgown on, an' her teeth was chatterin'. I took her into the bed, but it was an hour afore she could tell me onything, she was in sic a state.

"Sune after Hendry came in carryin' Joey. Joey was as naked as Leeby, and as cauld as lead, but he wasna greetin'. Instead o' that he was awfu' satisfied like, and for all Hendry threatened to lick him he wouldna tell what he an' Leeby had been doin'. He says, though, says he, 'Ye'll no gang awa noo, mother; no, ye'll bide noo.' My bonny laddie, I didna fathom him at the time.

"It was Leeby 'at I got it frae. Ye see, Joey had never seen me gaen ony gait withoot my staff, an' he thocht if he hod it I wouldna be able to gang awa. Ay, he planned it all oot, though he was but a bairn, an' lay watchin' me in my bed till I fell asleep. Syne he creepit oot o' the bed, an' got the staff, and gaed ben for Leeby. She was fleid, but he said it was the only wy to mak me 'at I couldna gang awa. It was juist ower there whaur thae cabbages is 'at he dug the hole wi' a spade, an' buried the staff. Hendry dug it up next mornin'."

Chapter 7

THE STATEMENT OF TIBBIE BIRSE

On a Thursday Pete Lownie was buried, and when Hendry returned from the funeral Jess asked if Davit Lunan had been there.

"Na," said Hendry, who was shut up in the closet-bed, taking off his blacks, "I heard tel he wasna bidden."

"Yea, yea," said Jess, nodding to me significantly. "Ay, weel," she added, "we'll be hae'n Tibbie ower here on Saturday to deve's (weary us) to death aboot it."

Tibbie, Davit's wife, was sister to Marget, Pete's widow, and she generally did visit Jess on Saturday night to talk about Marget, who was fast becoming one of the most fashionable persons in Thrums. Tibbie was hopelessly plebeian. She was none of your proud kind, and if I entered the kitchen when she was there she pretended not to see me, so that, if I chose, I might escape without speaking to the like of her. I always grabbed her hand, however, in a frank way.

On Saturday Tibbie made her appearance. From the rapidity of her walk, and the way she was sucking in her mouth, I knew that she had strange things to unfold. She had pinned a grey shawl about her shoulders, and wore a black mutch over her dangling grey curls.

"It's you, Tibbie," I heard Jess say, as the door opened.

Tibbie did not knock, not considering herself grand enough for ceremony, and indeed Jess would have resented her knocking. On the other hand, when Leeby visited Tibbie, she knocked as politely as if she were collecting for the precentor's present. All this showed that we were superior socially to Tibbie.

"Ay, hoo are ye, Jess?" Tibbie said.

"Muckle aboot it," answered Jess; "juist aff an' on; ay, an' hoo hae ye been yersel?"

"Ou," said Tibbie.

I wish I could write "ou" as Tibbie said it. With her it was usually a sentence in itself. Sometimes it was a mere bark, again it expressed indignation, surprise, rapture; it might be a check upon emotion or a way of leading up to it, and often it lasted for half a minute. In this instance it was, I should say, an intimation that if Jess was ready Tibbie would begin.

"So Pete Lownie's gone," said Jess, whom I could not see from ben the house. I had a good glimpse of Tibbie, however, through the open doorways. She had the armchair on the south side, as she would have said, of the fireplace.

"He's awa," assented Tibbie, primly.

I heard the lid of the kettle dancing, and then came a prolonged "ou." Tibbie bent forward to whisper, and if she had anything terrible to tell I was glad of that, for when she whispered I heard her best. For a time only a murmur of words reached me, distant music with an "ou" now and again that fired Tibbie as the beating of his drum may rouse the martial spirit of a drummer. At last our visitor broke into an agitated whisper, and it was only when she stopped whispering, as she did now and again, that I ceased to hear her. Jess evidently put a question at times, but so politely (for she had on her best wrapper) that I did not catch a word.

"Though I should be struck deid this nicht," Tibbie whispered, and the sibilants hissed between her few remaining teeth, "I wasna sae muckle as speared to the layin' oot. There was Mysy Cruickshanks there, an' Kitty Wobster 'at was nae friends to the corpse to speak o', but Marget passed by me, me 'at is her ain flesh an' blood, though it mayna be for the like o' me to say it. It's gospel truth, Jess, I tell ye, when I say 'at, for all I ken officially, as ye micht say, Pete Lownie may be weel and hearty this day. If I was to meet Marget in the face I couldna say he was deid, though I ken 'at the wricht coffined him; na, an' what's mair, I wouldna gie Marget the satisfaction o' hearin' me say it. No, Jess, I tell ye, I dinna pertend to be on an equalty wi' Marget, but equalty or no equalty, a body has her feelings, an' lat on 'at I ken Pete's gone I will not. Eh? Ou, weel . . .

"Na faags a; na, na. I ken my place better than to gang near Marget. I dinna deny 'at she's grand by me, an' her keeps a bakehoose o' her ain, an' glad am I to see her doin' sae weel, but let me tell ye this, Jess, 'Pride goeth before a fall.' Yes, it does, it's Scripture; ay, it's nae mak-up o' mine, it's Scripture. And this I will say, though kennin' my place, 'at Davit Lunan is as dainty a man as is in Thrums, an' there's no one 'at's better behaved at a bural, being particularly wise-like (presentable) in's blacks, an' them spleet new. Na, na, Jess, Davit may hae his faults an' tak a dram at times like anither, but he would shame naebody at a bural, an' Marget deleeberately insulted him, no speirin' him to Pete's. What's mair, when the minister cried in to see me yesterday, an' me on the floor washin', says he, 'So Marget's lost her man,' an' I said, 'Say ye so, na?' for let on 'at I kent, an' neither me at the layin' oot nor Davit Lunan at the funeral, I would not.

" 'David should hae gone to the funeral,' says the minister, 'for I doubt not he was only omitted in the invitations by a mistake.'

"Ay, it was weel meant, but says I, Jess, says I, 'As lang as am livin' to tak chairge o' 'im, Davit Lunan gangs to nae burals 'at he's no bidden to. An' I tell ye,' I says to the minister, 'if there was one body 'at had a richt to be at the bural o' Pete Lownie, it was Davit Lunan, him bein' my man an' Marget my ain sister. Yes, says I, though am no o' the boastin' kind, 'Davit had maist richt to be there next to Pete 'imsel. Ou, Jess . . .

"This is no a maiter I like to speak aboot; na, I dinna care to mention it, but the neighbours is nat'rally taen up aboot it, and Chirsty Tosh was sayin' what I would wager 'at Marget hadna sent the minister to hint 'at Davit's bein' over-lookit in the invitations was juist an accident? Losh, losh, Jess, to think 'at a woman could hae the michty assurance to mak a tool o' the very minister! But, sal, as far as that gangs, Marget would do it, an' gae twice to the kirk next Sabbath, too; but if she thinks she's to get ower me like that, she taks me for a bigger fule than I tak her for. Na, na, Marget, ye dinna draw my leg (deceive me). Ou, no . . .

"Mind ye, Jess, I hae no desire to be friends wi' Marget. Naething could be farrer frae my wish than to hae helpit in the layin' oot o' Pete Lownie, an', I assure ye, Davit wasna keen to gang to the bural. 'If they dinna want me to their burals,' Davit says, 'they hae nae mair to do than to say sae. But I warn ye, Tibbie,' he says, 'if there's a bural frae this hoose, be it your bural, or be it my bural, not one o' the family o' Lownies casts their shadows upon the corp.' Thae was the very words Davit said to me as we watched the hearse frae the sky-licht. Ay, he bore up wonderfu', but he felt it, Jess —he felt it, as I could tell by his takkin' to drink again that very nicht. Jess, Jess ...

"Marget's getting waur an' waur? Ay, ye may say so, though I'll say naething agin her mysel. Of coorse am no on equalty wi' her, especially since she had the bell put up in her hoose. Ou, I hinna seen it mysel, na, I never gang near the hoose, an', as mony a body can tell ye, when I do hae to gang that wy I mak my feet my friend. Ay, but as I was sayin', Marget's sae grand noo 'at she has a bell in the hoose. As I understan', there's a rope in the wast room, an' when ye pu' it a bell rings in the east room. Weel, when Marget has company at their tea in the wast room, an' they need mair watter or scones or onything, she rises an' rings the bell. Syne Jean, the auldest lassie, gets up frae the table an' lifts the jug or the plates an' gaes awa ben to the east room for what's wanted. Ay, it's a wy o' doin' 'at's juist like the gentry, but I'll tell ye, Jess, Pete juist fair hated the soond o' that bell, an' there's them 'at says it was the death o' 'im. To think o' Marget ha'en sic an establishment! ....

"Na, I hinna seen the mournin', I've heard o't. Na, if Marget doesna tell me naething, am no the kind to speir naething, an' though I'll be at the kirk the morn, I winna turn my heid to look at the mournin'. But it's fac as death I ken frae Janet McQuhatty 'at the bonnet's a' crape, an' three yairds o' crape on the dress, the which Marget calls a costume. . . . Ay, I wouldna wonder but what it was hale watter the morn, for it looks michty like rain, an' if it is it'll serve Marget richt, an' mebbe bring doon her pride a wee. No 'at I want to see, her humbled, for, in coorse, she's grand by the like o' me. Ou, but. . ."

Chapter 8

A CLOAK WITH BEADS

On weekdays the women who passed the window were meagrely dressed; mothers in draggled winsey gowns, carrying infants that were armfuls of grandeur. The Sabbath clothed every one in her best, and then the women went by with their hands spread out. When I was with Hendry cloaks with beads were the fashion, and Jess sighed as she looked at them. They were known in Thrums as the Eleven and a Bits (threepenny bits), that being their price at Kyowowy's in the square. Kyowowy means finicky, and applied to the draper by general consent. No doubt it was very characteristic to call the cloaks by their market value. In the glen my scholars still talk of their schoolbooks as the tupenny, the fowerpenny, the saxpenny. They finish their education with the tenpenny.

Jess's opportunity for handling the garments that others of her sex could finger in shops was when she had guests to tea. Persons who merely dropped in and remained to tea got their meal, as a rule, in the kitchen. They had nothing on that Jess could not easily take in as she talked to them. But when they came by special invitation, the meal was served in the room, the guests' things being left on the kitchen bed. Jess not being able to go ben the house, had to be left with the things. When the time to go arrived, these were found on the bed, just as they had been placed there, but Jess could now tell Leeby whether they were imitation, why Bell Elshioner's feather went far round the bonnet, and Chirsty Lownie's reason for always holding her left arm fast against her side when she went abroad in the black jacket. Ever since My Hobart's eleven and a bit was left on the kitchen bed Jess had hungered for a cloak with beads. My's was the very marrows of the one T'nowhead's wife got in Dundee for ten-and-sixpence; indeed, we would have thought that 'Lisbeth's also came from Kyowowy's had not Sanders Elshioner's sister seen her go into the Dundee shop with T'nowhead (who was loth), and hung about to discover what she was after.

Hendry was not quick at reading faces like Tammas Haggart, but the wistful look on Jess's face when there was talk of eleven and a bits had its meaning for him.

"They're grand to look at, no doubt," I have heard him say to Jess, "but they're richt annoyin'. That new wife o' Peter Dickie's had ane on in the kirk last Sabbath, an' wi' her sittin' juist afore us I couldna listen to the sermon for tryin' to count the beads."

Hendry made his way into these gossips uninvited, for his opinions on dress were considered contemptible, though he was worth consulting on material. Jess and Leeby discussed many things in his presence, confident that his ears were not doing their work; but every now and then it was discovered that he had been hearkening greedily. If the subject was dress, he might then become a little irritating.

"Oh, they're grand," Jess admitted; "they set a body aff oncommon."

"They would be no use to you," said Hendry, "for ye canna wear them except ootside."

"A body doesna buy cloaks to be wearin' at them steady," retorted Jess.

"No, no, but you could never wear yours though ye had ane."

"I dinna want ane. They're far ower grand for the like o' me."

"They're no nae sic thing. Am thinkin' ye're juist as fit to wear an eleven and a bit as My Hobart."

"Weel, mebbe I am, but it's oot o' the queistion gettin' ane, they're sic a price."

"Ay, an' though we had the siller, it would surely be an awfu' like thing to buy a cloak 'at ye could never wear?"

"Ou, but I dinna want ane."

Jess spoke so mournfully that Hendry became enraged.

"It's most michty," he said, " 'at ye would gang an' set yer heart on sic a completely useless thing."

"I hinna set my heart on't."

"Dinna blether. Ye've been speakin' aboot thae eleven and a bits to Leeby, aff an' on, for twa month."

Then Hendry hobbled off to his loom, and Jess gave me a look which meant that men are trying at the best, once you are tied to them.

The cloaks continued to turn up in conversation, and Hendry poured scorn upon Jess's weakness, telling her she would be better employed mending his trousers than brooding over an eleven and a bit that would have to spend its life in a drawer. An outsider would have thought that Hendry was positively cruel to Jess. He seemed to take a delight in finding that she had neglected to sew a button on his waistcoat. His real joy, however, was the knowledge that she sewed as no other woman in Thrums could sew. Jess had a genius for making new garments out of old ones, and Hendry never tired of gloating over her cleverness so long as she was not present. He was always athirst for fresh proofs of it, and these were forthcoming every day. Sparing were his words of praise to herself, but in the evening he generally had a smoke with me in the attic, and then the thought of Jess made him chuckle till his pipe went out. When he smoked he grunted as if in pain, though this really added to the enjoyment.

"It doesna matter," he would say to me, "what Jess turns her hand to, she can mak ony mortal thing. She doesna need nae teachin'; na, juist gie her a guid look at onything, be it clothes, or furniture, or in the bakin' line, it's all the same to her. She'll mak another exactly like it. Ye canna beat her. Her bannocks is so superior 'at a Tilliedrum woman took to her bed after tastin' them, an' when the lawyer has company his wife gets Jess to mak some bannocks for her an' syne pretends they're her ain bakin'. Ay, there's a story aboot that. One day the auld doctor, him 'at's deid, was at his tea at the lawyer's, an' says the guidwife, 'Try the cakes, Mr.

Riach; they're my own bakin'.' Weel, he was a fearsomely outspoken man, the doctor, an' nae suner had he the bannock atween his teeth, for he didna stop to swallow't, than he says, 'Mistress Geddie,' says he, 'I wasna born on a Sabbath. Na, na, you're no the first grand leddy 'at has gien me bannocks as their ain bakin' 'at was baked and fired by Jess Logan, her 'at's Hendry McQumpha's wife.' Ay, they say the lawyer's wife didna ken which wy to look, she was that mortified. It's juist the same wi' sewin'. There's wys o' ornamentin' christenin' robes an' the like 'at's kent to naebody but herself; an' as for stockin's, weel, though I've seen her mak sae mony, she amazes me yet. I mind o' a furry waistcoat I aince had. Weel, when it was fell dune, do you think she gae it awa to some gaen aboot body (vagrant)? Na, she made it into a richt neat coat to Jamie, wha was a bit laddie at the time. When he grew out o' it, she made a slipbody o't for hersel. Ay, I dinna ken a' the different things it became, but the last time I saw it was ben in the room, whaur she'd covered a footstool wi' 't. Yes, Jess is the cleverest crittur I ever saw. Leeby's handy, but she's no a patch on her mother."

I sometimes repeated these panegyrics to Jess. She merely smiled, and said that men haver most terrible when they are not at their work.

Hendry tried Jess sorely over the cloaks, and a time came when, only by exasperating her could he get her to reply to his sallies.

"Wha wants an eleven an' a bit?" she retorted now and again.

"It's you 'at wants it," said Hendry, promptly.

"Did I ever say I wanted ane? What use could I hae for't?"

"That's the queistion," said Hendry. "Ye canna gang the length o' the door, so ye would never be able to wear't."

"Ay, weel," replied Jess, "I'll never hae the chance o' no bein' able to wear't, for, hooever muckle I wanted it, I couldna get it."

Jess's infatuation had in time the effect of making Hendry uncomfortable. In the attic he delivered himself of such sentiments as these:

"There's nae understandin' a woman. There's Jess 'at hasna her equal for cleverness in Thrums, man or woman, an' yet she's fair skeered about thae cloaks. Aince a woman sets her mind on something to wear, she's mair onreasonable than the stupidest man. Ay, it micht mak them humble to see hoo foolish they are syne. No, but it doesna do't.

"If it was a thing to be useful noo, I wouldna think the same o't, but she could never wear't. She kens she could never wear't, an' yet she's juist as keen to hae't.

"I dinna like to see her so wantin' a thing, an' no able to get it. But it's an awfu' sum, eleven an' a bit."

He tried to argue with her further.

"If ye had eleven an' a bit to fling awa," he said, "ye dinna mean to tell me 'at ye would buy a cloak instead o' cloth for a gown, or flannel for petticoats, or some useful thing?"

"As sure as death," said Jess, with unwonted vehemence, "if a cloak I could get, a cloak I would buy."

Hendry came up to tell me what Jess had said.

"It's a michty infatooation," he said, "but it shows hoo her heart's set on thae cloaks."

"Aince ye had it," he argued with her, "ye would juist hae to lock it awa in the drawers. Ye, would never even be seein' 't."

"Ay, would I," said Jess. " I would often tak it oot an' look at it. Ay, an' I would aye ken it was there."

"But naebody would ken ye had it but yersel," said Hendry, who had a vague notion that this was a telling objection.

"Would they no?" answered Jess. " It would be a' through the toon afore nicht."

"Weel, all I can say," said Hendry, "is 'at ye're terrible foolish to tak the want o' sic a useless thing to heart."

"Am no takkin' 't to heart," retorted Jess, as usual.

Jess needed many things in her days that poverty kept from her to the end, and the cloak was merely a luxury. She would soon have let it slip by as something unattainable had not Hendry encouraged it to rankle in her mind. I cannot say when he first determined that Jess should have a cloak, come the money as it liked, for he was too ashamed of his weakness to admit his project to me. I remember, however, his saying to Jess one day:

"I'll warrant ye could mak a cloak yersel the marrows o' thae eleven and a bits, at half the price?"

"It would cost," said Jess, "sax an' saxpence, exactly. The, cloth would be five shillins, an' the beads a shillin'. I have some braid 'at would do fine for the front, but the buttons would be saxpence."

"Ye're sure o' that?"

"I ken fine, for I got Leeby to price the things in the shop."

"Ay, but it maun be ill to shape the cloaks richt. There was a queer cut aboot that ane Peter Dickie's new wife had on."

"Queer cut or no queer cut," said Jess, "I took the shape o' My Hobart's ane the day she was here at her tea, an' I could mak the identical o't for sax an' sax."

"I dinna believe't," said Hendry, but when he and I were alone he told me, "There's no a doubt she could mak it. Ye heard her say she had taen the shape? Ay, that shows she's rale set on a cloak."

Had Jess known that Hendry had been saving up for months to buy her material for a cloak, she would not have let him do it. She could not know, however, for all the time he was scraping together his pence, he kept up a ring-ding-dang about her folly. Hendry gave Jess all the wages he weaved, except threepence weekly, most of which went in tobacco and snuff. The dulseman had perhaps a halfpenny from him in the fortnight. I noticed that for a long time Hendry neither smoked nor snuffed, and I knew that for years he had carried a shilling in his snuff-mull. The remainder of the money he must have made by extra work at his loom, by working harder, for he could scarcely have worked longer.

It was one day shortly before Jamie's return to Thrums that Jess saw Hendry pass the house and go down the brae when he ought to have come in to his brose. She sat at the window watching for him, and by and by he reappeared, carrying a parcel.

"Whaur on earth hae ye been?" she asked, "an' what's that you're carryin'?"

"Did ye think it was an eleven an' a bit?" said Hendry.

"No, I didna," answered Jess, indignantly.

Then Hendry slowly undid the knots of the string with which the parcel was tied. He took off the brown paper.

"There's yer cloth," he said, "an' here's one an' saxpence for the beads an' the buttons."

While Jess still stared he followed me ben the house.

"It's a terrible haver," he said, apologetically, "but she had set her heart on't."

Chapter 9

THE POWER OF BEAUTY

One evening there was such a gathering at the pig-sty that Hendry and I could not get a board to lay our backs against. Circumstances had pushed Pete Elshioner into the place of honour that belonged by right of mental powers to Tammas Haggart, and Tammas was sitting rather sullenly on the bucket, boring a hole in the pig with his sarcastic eye. Pete was passing round a card, and in time it reached me. "With Mr. and Mrs. David Alexander's compliments," was printed on it, and Pete leered triumphantly at us as it went the round.

"Weel, what think ye?" he asked, with a pretence at modesty.

"Ou," said T'nowhead, looking at the others like one who asked a question, "ou, I think; ay, ay."

The others seemed to agree with him, all but Tammas, who did not care to tie himself down to an opinion.

"Ou ay," T'nowhead continued, more confidently, "it is so, deceededly."

"Ye'll no ken," said Pete, chuckling, " what it means?"

"Na," the farmer admitted, "na, I canna say I exac'ly ken that."

"I ken, though," said Tammas, in his keen way.

"Weel, then, what is't?" demanded Pete, who had never properly come under Tammas's spell.

"I ken," said Tammas.

"Oot wi't then."

"I dinna say it's lyin' on my tongue," Tammas replied, in a tone of reproof, "but if ye'll juist speak awa aboot some other thing for a meenute or twa, I'll tell ye syne."

Hendry said that this was only reasonable, but we could think of no subject at the moment, so we only stared at Tammas, and waited.

"I fathomed it", he said at last, "as sune as my een lichted on't. It's one o' the bit cards 'at grand fowk slip 'aneath doors when they mak calls, an their friends is no in. Ay, that's what it is."

"I dinna say ye're wrang," Pete answered, a little annoyed. "Ay, weel, lads, of course David Alexander's oor Dite as we called 'im, Dite Elshioner, an' that's his wy o' signifyin' to us 'at he's married."

"I assure ye," said Hendry, "Dite's doin' the thing in style."

"Ay, we said that when the card arrived," Pete admitted.

"I kent," said Tammas, " 'at that was the wy grand fowk did when they got married. I've kent it a lang time. It's no nae surprise to me."

"He's been lang in marryin'," Hockey Crewe said.

"He was thirty at Martinmas," said Pete.

"Thirty, was he?" said Hockey. "Man, I'd buried twa wives by the time I was that age, an' was castin' aboot for a third."

"I mind o' them," Hendry interposed.

"Ay," Hockey said, the first twa was angels."

There he paused. "An' so's the third," he added, "in many respects."

"But wha's the woman Dite's ta'en?" T'nowhead or some one of the more silent members of the company asked of Pete.

"Ou, we dinna ken wha she is," answered Pete; "but she'll be some Glasca lassie, for he's there noo. Look, lads, look at this. He sent this at the same time; it's her picture." Pete produced the silhouette of a young lady, and handed it round.

"What do ye think? " he asked.

"I assure ye!" said Hookey.

"Sal," said Hendry, even more charmed, "Dite's done weel."

"Lat's see her in a better licht," said Tammas.

He stood up and examined the photograph narrowly, while Pete fidgeted with his legs.

"Fairish," said Tammas at last. "Ou, ay; no what I would selec' mysel, but a dainty bit stocky! Ou, a tasty crittury! ay, an' she's weel in order. Lads, she's a fine stoot kimmer."

"I conseeder her a beauty," said Pete, aggressively.

"She's a' that," said Hendry.

"A' I can say," said Hookey, "is 'at she taks me most michty."

"She's no a beauty," Tammas maintained; "na, she doesna juist come up to that; but I dinna deny but what she's weel faured."

"What faut do ye find wi' her, Tammas?" asked Hendry.

"Conseedered critically," said Tammas, holding the photograph at arm's length, "I would say 'at she — let's see noo; ay, I would say 'at she's defeecient in genteelity."

"Havers," said Pete.

"Na," said Tammas, "no when conseedered critically. Ye see she's drawn lauchin'; an' the genteel thing's no to lauch, but juist to put on a bit smirk. Ay, that's the genteel thing."

"A smile, they ca' it," interposed T'nowhead.

"I said a smile," continued Tammas. "Then there's her waist. I say naething agin her waist, speakin' in the ord'nar meanin'; but, conseedered critically, there's a want o' suppleness, as ye micht say, aboot it. Ay, it doesna compare wi' the waist o' — " (Here Tammas mentioned a young lady who had recently married into a local county family.)

"That was a pretty tiddy," said Hookey. "Ou, losh, ay! it made me a kind o' queery to look at her."

"Ye're ower kyowowy (particular), Tammas," said Pete.

"I may be, Pete," Tammas admitted; "but I maun say I'm fond o' a bonny-looken wuman, an' no aisy to please: na, I'm nat'rally ane o' the critical kind."

"It's extror'nar," said T'nowhead, "what a poo'er beauty has. I mind when I was a callant readin' aboot Mary Queen o' Scots till I was fair mad, lads; yes, I was fair mad at her bein' deid. Ou, I could hardly sleep at nichts for thinking o' her."

"Mary was spunky as weel as a beauty," said Hookey, "an' that's the kind I like. Lads, what a persuasive tid she was!"

"She got roond the men," said Hendry, "ay, she turned them roond her finger. That's the warst o' thae beauties."

"I dinna gainsay," said T'nowhead, "but what there was a little o' the deevil in Mary, the crittur."

Here T'nowhead chuckled, and then looked scared.

"What Mary needed," said Tammas, "was a strong man to manage her."

"Ay, man, but it's ill to manage thae beauties. They gie ye a glint o' their een, an' syne whaur are ye?"

"Ah, they can be managed," said Tammas, complacently. "There's naebody nat'rally safter wi' a pretty stocky o' a bit wumany than mysel; but for a' that, if I had been Mary's man I would hae stood nane o' her tantrums. 'Na, Mary, my lass,' I would hae said, 'this winna do; na, na, ye're a bonny body, but ye maun mind 'at man's the superior; ay, man's the lord o' creation, an' so ye maun juist sing sma'.' That's hoo I would hae managed Mary, the speerity crittur 'at she was."

"Ye would hae haen yer wark cut oot for ye, Tammas."

"Ilka mornin'," pursued Tammas, "I would hae said to her, 'Mary,' I would hae said, 'wha's to wear thae breeks the day, you or me?' Ay, syne I would hae ordered her to kindle the fire, or if I had been the king, of coorse I would hae telt her instead to ring the bell an' hae the cloth laid for the breakfast. Ay, that's the wy to mak the like o' Mary respec ye."

Pete and I left them talking. He had written a letter to David Alexander, and wanted me to "back" it.

Chapter 10

A MAGNUM OPUS

Two Bibles, a volume of sermons by the learned Dr. Isaac Barrow, a few numbers of the *Cheap Magazine*, that had strayed from Dunfermline, and a *Pilgrim's Progress*, were the works that lay conspicuous ben in the room. Hendry had also a copy of Burns, whom he always quoted in the complete poem, and a collection of legends in song and prose, that Leeby kept out of sight in a drawer.

The weight of my box of books was a subject Hendry was very willing to shake his head over, but he never showed any desire to take off the lid. Jess, however, was more curious; indeed, she would have been an omnivorous devourer of books had it not been for her conviction that reading was idling.

Until I found her out she never allowed to me that Leeby brought her my books one at a time. Some of them were novels, and Jess took about ten minutes to each. She confessed that what she read was only the last chapter, owing to a consuming curiosity to know whether "she got him."

She read all the London part, however, of *The Heart of Midlothian*, because London was where Jamie lived, and she and I had a discussion about it which ended in her remembering that Thrums once had an author of its own.

"Bring oot the book," she said to Leeby, "it was put awa i' the bottom drawer ben i' the room sax year syne, an' I sepad it's there yet."

Leeby came but with a faded little book, the title already rubbed from its shabby brown covers. I opened it, and then all at once I saw before me again the man who wrote and printed it and died. He came hobbling up the brae, so bent that his body was almost at right angles to his legs, and his broken silk hat was carefully brushed as in the days when Janet, his sister, lived. There he stood at the top of the brae, panting.

I was but a boy when Jimsy Duthie turned the corner of the brae for the last time, with a score of mourners behind him. While I knew him there was no Janet to run to the door to see if he was coming. So occupied was Jimsy with the great affair of his life, which was brewing for thirty years, that his neighbours saw how he missed his sister better than he realized it himself. Only his hat was no longer carefully brushed, and his coat hung awry, and there was sometimes little reason why he should go home to dinner. It is for the sake of Janet who adored him that we should remember Jimsy in the days before she died.

Jimsy was a poet, and for the space of thirty years he lived in a great epic on the Millennium. This is the book presented to me by Jess, that lies so quietly on my topmost shelf now. Open it, however, and you will find that the work is entitled "The Millennium: an Epic Poem, in Twelve Books: by James Duthie." In the little hole in his wall where Jimsy kept his books there was, I have no doubt—for his effects were rouped before I knew him except by name— a well-read copy of *Paradise Lost*. Some people would smile, perhaps, if they read the two epics side by side, and others might sigh, for there is a great deal in "The Millennium" that Milton could take credit for. Jimsy had educated himself, after the idea of writing something that the world would not willingly let die came to him, and he began his book before his education was complete. So far as I know, he never wrote a line that had not to do with "The Millennium." He was ever a man sparing of his plural tenses, and "The Millennium" says "has" for "have"; a vain word, indeed, which Thrums would only have permitted as a poetical license. The one original character in the poem is the devil, of whom Jimsy gives a picture that is startling and graphic, and received the approval of the Auld Licht minister.

By trade Jimsy was a printer, a master-printer with no one under him, and he printed and bound his book, ten copies in all, as well as wrote it. To print the poem took him, I dare say, nearly as long as to write it, and he set up the pages as they were written, one by one. The book is only printed on one side of the leaf, and each page was produced separately like a little hand-bill. Those who may pick up the book—but who will care to do so? — will think that the author or his printer could not spell but they would not do Jimsy that injustice if they knew the circumstances in which it was produced. He had but a small stock of type, and on many occasions he ran out of a letter. The letter *e* tried him sorely. Those who knew him best say that he tried to think of words without an *e* in them, but when he was baffled he had to use a little *a* or an *o* instead. He could print correctly, but in the book there are a good many capital letters in the middle of words, and sometimes there is a note of interrogation after "Alas" or "Woes me," because all the notes of exclamation had been used up.

Jimsy never cared to speak about his great poem even to his closest friends, but Janet told how he read it out to her, and that his whole body trembled with excitement while he raised his eyes to heaven as if asking for inspiration that would enable his voice to do justice to his writing. So grand it was, said Janet, that her stocking would slip from her fingers as he read and Janet's stockings, that she was always knitting when not otherwise engaged, did not slip from her hands readily. After her death he was heard by his neighbours reciting the poem to himself, generally with his door locked. He is said to have declaimed part of it one still evening from the top of the commonty like one addressing a multitude, and the idlers who had crept up to jeer at him fell back when they saw his face. He walked through them, they told, with his old body straight once more, and a queer light playing on his face. His lips are moving as I see him turning the corner of the brae. So he passed from youth to old age, and all his life seemed a dream, except that part of it in which he was writing, or printing, or stitching, or binding "The Millennium." At last the work was completed.

"It is finished," he printed at the end of the last book. " The task of thirty years is over."

It is indeed over. No one ever read "The Millennium." I am not going to sentimentalize over my copy, for how much of it have I read? But neither shall I say that it was written to no end.

You may care to know the last of Jimsy, though in one sense he was blotted out when the last copy was bound. He had saved one hundred pounds by that time, and being now neither able to work nor to live alone, his friends cast about for a home for his remaining years. He was very spent and feeble, yet he had the fear that he might be still alive when all his money was gone. After that was the workhouse. He covered sheets of paper with calculations about how long the hundred pounds would last if he gave away for board and lodgings ten shillings, nine shillings, seven and sixpence a week. At last, with sore misgivings, he went to live with a family who took him for eight shillings. Less than a month afterwards he died.

Chapter 11

THE GHOST CRADLE

Our dinner-hour was twelve o'clock, and Hendry, for a not incomprehensible reason, called this meal his brose. Frequently, however, while I was there to share the expense, broth was put on the table, with beef to follow in clean plates, much to Hendry's distress, for the comfortable and usual practice was to eat the beef from the broth-plates. Jess, however, having three whole white plates and two cracked ones, insisted on the meals being taken genteelly, and her husband, with a look at me, gave way.

"Half a pound o' boiling beef, an' a penny bone," was Leeby's almost invariable order when she dealt with the flesher, and Jess had always neighbours poorer than herself who got a plateful of the broth. She never had anything without remembering some old body who would be the better of a little of it.

Among those who must have missed Jess sadly after she was gone was Johnny Proctor, a halfwitted man who, because he could not work, remained straight at a time of life when most weavers, male and female had lost some inches of their stature. For as far back as my memory goes, Johnny had got his brose three times a week from Jess, his custom being to walk in without ceremony, and, drawing a stool to the table, tell Leeby that he was now ready. One day, however, when I was in the garden putting some rings on a fishing-wand, Johnny pushed by me, with no sign of recognition on his face. I addressed him, and, after pausing undecidedly, he ignored me. When he came to the door, instead of flinging it open and walking in, he knocked primly, which surprised me so much that I followed him.

"Is this whaur Mistress McQumpha lives?" he asked, when Leeby, with a face ready to receive the minister himself, came at length to the door.

I knew that the gentility of the knock had taken both her and her mother aback.

"Hoots, Johnny," said Leeby, "what haver's this ? Come awa in."

Johnny seemed annoyed.

"Is this whaur Mistress McQumpha lives?" he repeated.

"Say 'at it is," cried Jess, who was quicker in the uptake than her daughter.

"Of course this is whaur Mistress McQumpha lives," Leeby then said, "as weel ye ken, for ye had yer dinner here no twa hours syne."

"Then," said Johnny, "Mistress Tully's compliments to her, and would she kindly lend the christenin' robe, an' also the tea-tray, if the same be na needed?"

Having delivered his message as instructed, Johnny consented to sit down until the famous christening robe and the tray were ready, but he would not talk, for that was not in the bond. Jess's sweet face beamed over the compliment Mrs. Tully, known on ordinary occasions as Jean McTaggart, had paid her, and, after Johnny had departed laden, she told me how the tray, which had a great bump in the middle, came into her possession.

"Ye've often heard me speak aboot the time when I was a lassie workin' at the farm o' the Bog? Ay, that was afore me an' Hendry kent ane anither, an' I was as fleet on my feet in thae days as Leeby is noo. It was Sam'l Fletcher 'at was the farmer, but he maun hae been gone afore you was mair than born. Mebbe, though, ye ken 'at he was a terrible invalid, an' for the hinmost years o' his life he sat in a muckle chair nicht an' day. Ay, when I took his denner to 'im, on that very tray 'at Johnny cam for, I little thocht 'at by an' by I would be sae keepit in a chair mysel.

"But the thinkin' o' Sam'l Fletcher's case is ane o' the things 'at maks me awfu' thankfu' for the lenient wy the Lord has aye dealt wi' me; for Sam'l couldna move oot o' the chair, aye sleepin' in't at nicht, an' I can come an' gang between mine an' my bed. Mebbe, ye think I'm no much better off than Sam'l, but that's a terrible mistak.

What a glory it would hae been to him if he could hae gone frae ane end o' the kitchen to the ither. Ay, I'm sure o' that.

"Sam'l was rale weel liked, for he was saft-spoken to everybody, an' fond o' ha'en a gossip wi' ony ane 'at was aboot the farm. We didna care sae muckle for the wife, Eppie Lownie, for she managed the farm, an' she was fell hard an' terrible reserved we thocht, no even likin' ony body to get friendly wi' the mester, as we called Sam'l. Ay, we made a richt mistak."

As I had heard frequently of this queer, mournful mistake made by those who considered Sam'l unfortunate in his wife, I turned Jess on to the main line of her story.

"It was the ghost cradle, as they named it, 'at I meant to tell ye aboot. The Bog was a bigger farm in thae days than noo, but I daursay it has the new steadin' yet. Ay, it winna be new noo, but at the time there was sic a commotion aboot the ghost cradle, they were juist puttin' the new steadin' up. There was sax or mair masons at it, wi' the lads on the farm helpin', an' as they were all sleepin' at the farm, there was great stir aboot the place. I couldna tell ye hoo the story aboot the farm's bein' haunted rose, to begin wi', but I mind fine hoo fleid I was; ay, an' no only me, but every man-body an' woman-body on the farm. It was aye late 'at the soond began, an' we never saw naething, we juist heard it. The masons said they wouldna hae been sae fleid if they could hae seen't, but it never was seen. It had the soond o' a cradle rockin', an' when we lay in our beds hearkenin', it grew louder an' louder till it wasna to be borne, an' the women-folk fair skirled wi' fear. The mester was intimate wi' a' the stories aboot ghosts an' water-kelpies an' sic like, an' we couldna help listenin' to them. But he aye said 'at ghosts 'at was juist heard an' no seen was the maist fearsome an' wicked. For all there was sic fear ower the hale farm-toon 'at naebody would gang ower the door alane after the gloamin' cam, the mester said he wasna fleid to sleep i' the kitchen by 'imsel. We thocht it richt brave o' 'im, for ye see he was as helpless as a bairn.

"Richt queer stories rose aboot the cradle, an' travelled to the ither farms. The wife didna like them ava, for it was said 'at there maun hae been some awful murder o' an infant on the farm, or we wouldna be haunted by a cradle. Syne folk began to mind 'at there had been nae bairns born on the farm as far back as onybody kent, an' it was said 'at some lang syne crime had made the Bog cursed.

"Dinna think 'at we juist lay in our beds or sat round the fire shakkin' wi' fear. Everything 'at could be dune was dune. In the daytime, when naething was heard, the masons explored a' place i' the farm, in the hope o' findin' oot 'at the sound was caused by sic a thing as the wind playin' on the wood in the garret. Even at nichts, when they couldna sleep wi' the soond, I've kent them rise in a body an' gang all ower the house wi' lichts. I've seen them climbin' on the new steadin', crawlin' alang the rafters haudin' their cruizey lamps afore them, an' us women-bodies shiverin' wi' fear at the door. It was on ane o' thae nichts 'at a mason fell off the rafters an' broke his leg. Weel, sic a state was the men in to find oot what it was 'at was terrifyin' them sae muckle, 'at the rest o' them climbed up at aince to the place he'd fallen frae, thinkin' there was something there 'at had fleid 'im. But though they crawled back an' forrit there was naething ava.

"The rockin' was louder, we thocht, after that nicht, an' syne the men said it would go on till somebody was killed. That idea took a richt haud o' them, an' twa ran awa back to Tilliedrum, whaur they had come frae. They gaed thegither the middle o' the nicht, an' it was thocht next mornin' 'at the ghost had spirited them awa.

"Ye couldna conceive hoo low-spirited we all were after the masons had gien up hope o' findin' a nat'ral cause for the soond. At ord'nar times there's no ony mair lichtsome place than a farm after the men hae come in to their supper, but at the Bog we sat dour an' sullen; an' there wasna a mason or a farm-servant 'at would gang by 'imsel as far as the end o' the hoose whaur the peats was keepit. The mistress maun hae saved some siller that spring through the Egyptians (gypsies) keepin' awa, for the farm had got sic an ill name, 'at nae tinkler would come near't at nicht. The tailorman an' his laddie, 'at should hae bidden wi' us to sew things for the men, walkit off fair skeered one mornin', an' settled doon at the farm o' Cragiebuckle fower mile awa, whaur our lads had to gae to them. Ay, I mind the tailor's sendin' the laddie for the money owin' him; he hadna the speerit to venture again within soond o' the cradle 'imsel. The men on the farm, though, couldna blame 'im for that. They were juist as flichtered themsels, an' mony a time I saw them hittin' the dogs for whinin' at the soond. The wy the dogs took on was fearsome in itsel, for they seemed to ken, aye when nicht cam on, 'at the rockin' would sune begin, an' if they werena chained they cam runnin' to the hoose. I hae heard the hale glen fu, as ye micht say, wi' the whinin' o' dogs, for the dogs on the other farms took up the cry, an' in a glen ye can hear soonds terrible far awa at nicht.

"As lang as we sat i' the kitchen listenin' to what the mester had to say aboot the ghosts in his young days, the cradle would be still, but we were nae suner awa speeritless to our beds than it began, an sometimes it lasted till mornin'. We lookit upon the mester almost wi' awe, sittin' there sae helpless in his chair, an' no fleid to be left alane. He had lang white hair, an' a saft bonny face 'at would hae made 'im respeckit by onybody, an' aye when we speired if he wasna fleid to be left alane, he said, 'Them 'at has a clear conscience has naething to fear frae ghosts.'

"There was some 'at said the curse would never leave the farm till the house was razed to the ground, an' it's the truth I'm tellin' ye when I say there was talk among the men aboot settin't on fire. The mester was richt stern when he heard o' that, quotin' frae Scripture in a solemn wy 'at abashed the masons, but he said 'at in his opeenion there was a bairn buried on the farm, an' till it was found the cradle would go on rockin'. After that the masons dug in a lot o' places lookin' for the body, an' they found some queer things, too, but never nae sign o' a murdered litlin'. Ay, I dinna ken what would hae happened if the commotion had gaen on muckle langer. One thing I'm sure o' is 'at the mistress would hae gaen daft, she took it a' sae terrible to heart.

"I lauch at it noo, but I tell ye I used to tak my heart to my bed in my mooth. If ye hinna heard the story, I dinna think ye'll be able to guess what the ghost cradle was."

I said I had been trying to think what the tray had to do with it.

"It had everything to do wi't," said Jess "an' if the masons had kent hoo that cradle was, rockit, I think they would hae killed the mester. It was Eppie 'at found oot, an' she telt naebody but me, though mony a ane kens noo. I see ye canna mak it oot yet, so I'll tell ye what the cradle was. The tray was keepit against the kitchen wall near the mester, an' he played on't wi' his foot. He made it gang bump bump, an' the soond was juist like a cradle rockin'. Ye could hardly believe sic a thing would hae made that din, but it did, an' ye see we lay in our beds hearkening for't. Ay, when Eppie telt me, I could scarce believe 'at that guid devout-lookin' man could hae been sae wicked. Ye see, when he found hoo terrified we a' were, he keepit it up. The wy Eppie found out i' the tail o' the day was by wonderin' at 'im sleepin' sae muckle in the daytime. He did that so as to be fresh for his sport at nicht. What a fine releegious man we thocht 'im, too!

"Eppie couldna bear the very sicht o' the tray after that, an' she telt me to break it up; but I keepit it, ye see. The lump i' the middle's the mark, as ye may say, o' the auld man's foot."

Chapter 12

THE TRAGEDY OF A WIFE

Were Jess still alive to tell the life-story of Sam'l Fletcher and his wife, you could not hear it and sit still. The ghost cradle is but a page from the black history of a woman who married, to be blotted out from that hour. One case of the kind I myself have known, of a woman so good mated to a man so selfish that I cannot think of her even now with a steady mouth. Hers was the tragedy of living on, more mournful than the tragedy that kills. In Thrums the weavers spoke of "lousing" from their looms, removing the chains, and there is something woeful in that. But pity poor Nanny Coutts, who took her chains to bed with her.

Nanny was buried a month or more before I came to the house on the brae, and even in Thrums the dead are seldom remembered for so long a time as that. But it was only after Sanders was left alone that we learned what a woman she had been, and how basely we had wronged her. She was an angel, Sanders went about whining when he had no longer a woman to ill-treat. He had this sentimental way with him, but it lost its effect after we knew the man.

"A deevil couldna hae deserved waur treatment," Tammas Haggart said to him; "gang oot o' my sicht, man."

"I'll blame mysel till I die," Jess said, with tears in her eyes, " for no understandin' puir Nanny better."

So Nanny got sympathy at last, but not until her forgiving soul had left her tortured body. There was many a kindly heart in Thrums that would have gone out to her in her lifetime, but we could not have loved her without upbraiding him, and she would not buy sympathy at the price. What a little story it is, and how few words are required to tell it! He was a bad husband to her, and she kept it secret. That is Nanny's life summed up. It is all that was left behind when her coffin went down the brae. Did she love him to the end, or was she only doing what she thought her duty? It is not for me even to guess. A good woman who suffers is altogether beyond man's reckoning. To such heights of self-sacrifice we cannot rise. It crushes us; it ought to crush us on to our knees. For us who saw Nanny, infirm, shrunken, and so weary, yet a type of the noblest womanhood, suffering for years, and misunderstood her to the end, what expiation can there be? I do not want to storm at the man who made her life so burdensome. Too many years have passed for that, nor would Nanny take it kindly if I called her man names.

Sanders worked little after his marriage. He had a sore back, he said, which became a torture if he leant forward at his loom. What truth there was in this I cannot say, but not every weaver in Thrums could "louse" when his back grew sore. Nanny went to the loom in his place, filling as well as weaving, and he walked about, dressed better than the common, and with cheerful words for those who had time to listen. Nanny got no approval even for doing his work as well as her own, for they were understood to have money, and Sanders let us think her merely greedy. We drifted into his opinions.

Had Jess been one of those who could go about, she would, I think, have read Nanny better than the rest of us, for her intellect was bright, and always led her straight to her neighbours' hearts. But Nanny visited no one, and so Jess only knew her by hearsay. Nanny's standoffishness, as it was called, was not a popular virtue, and she was blamed still more for trying to keep her husband out of other people's houses. He was so frank and full of gossip, and she was so reserved. He would go everywhere, and she nowhere. He had been known to ask neighbours to tea, and she had shown that she wanted them away, or even begged them not to come. We were not accustomed to go behind the face of a thing, and so we set down Nanny's inhospitality to churlishness or greed. Only after her death, when other women had to attend him, did we get to know what a tyrant Sanders was at his own hearth. The ambition of Nanny's life was that we should never know it, that we should continue extolling him, and say what we chose about herself. She knew that if we went much about the house and saw how he treated her, Sanders would cease to be a respected man in Thrums.

So neat in his dress was Sanders, that he was seldom seen abroad in corduroys. His blue bonnet for everyday wear was such as even well-to-do farmers only wore at fair-time, and it was said that he had a handkerchief for every day in the week. Jess often held him up to Hendry as a model of courtesy and polite manners.

"Him an' Nanny's no weel matched," she used to say, "for he has grand ideas, an' she's o' the commonest. It maun be a richt trial to a man wi' his fine tastes to hae a wife 'at's wrapper's never even on, an' wha doesna wash her mutch aince in a month."

It is true that Nanny was a slattern, but only because she married into slavery. She was kept so busy washing and ironing for Sanders that she ceased to care how she looked herself. What did it matter whether her mutch was clean? Weaving and washing and cooking, doing the work of a breadwinner as well as of a housewife, hers was soon a body prematurely old, on which no wrapper would sit becomingly. Before her face, Sanders would hint that her slovenly ways and dress tried him sorely, and in company at least she only bowed her head. We were given to respecting those who worked hard, but Nanny, we thought, was a woman of means, and Sanders let us call her a miser. He was always anxious, he said, to be generous, but Nanny would not let him assist a starving child. They had really not a penny beyond what Nanny earned at the loom, and now we know how Sanders shook her if she did not earn enough. His vanity was responsible for the story about her wealth, and she would not have us think him vain.

Because she did so much, we said that she was as strong as a cart-horse. The doctor who attended her during the last week of her life discovered that she had never been well. Yet we had often wondered at her letting Sanders pit his own potatoes when he was so unable.

"Them 'at's strong, ye see," Sanders explained, "doesna ken what illness is, an' so it's nat'ral they shouldna sympathize wi' onweel fowk.

Ay, I'm rale thankfu' 'at Nanny keeps her health. I often envy her."

These were considered creditable sentiments, and so they might have been had Nanny uttered them. Thus easily Sanders built up a reputation for never complaining. I know now that he was a hard and cruel man who should have married a shrew; but while Nanny lived I thought he had a beautiful nature. Many a time I have spoken with him at Hendry's gate, and felt the better of his heartiness.

"I mauna complain," he always said; "na, we maun juist fecht awa."

Little, indeed, had he to complain of, and little did he fight away.

Sanders went twice to church every Sabbath, and thrice when he got the chance. There was no man who joined so lustily in the singing or looked straighter at the minister during the prayer. I have heard the minister say that Sanders's constant attendance was an encouragement and a help to him. Nanny had been a great church-goer when she was a maiden, but after her marriage she only went in the afternoons, and a time came when she ceased altogether to attend. The minister admonished her many times, telling her, among other things, that her irreligious ways were a distress to her husband. She never replied that she could not go to church in the forenoon because Sanders insisted on a hot meal being waiting him when the service ended. But it was true that Sanders, for appearances' sake, would have had her go to church in the afternoons. It is now believed that on this point alone did she refuse to do as she was bidden. Nanny was very far from perfect, and the reason she forsook the kirk utterly was because she had no Sabbath clothes.

She died as she had lived, saying not a word when the minister, thinking it his duty, drew a cruel comparison between her life and her husband's.

"I got my first glimpse into the real state of affairs in that house," the doctor told me one night on the brae, "the day before she died. 'You're sure there's no hope for me?' she asked wistfully, and when I had to tell the truth she sank back on the pillow with a look of joy."

Nanny died with a lie on her lips. "Ay," she said, "Sanders has been a guid man to me."

Chapter 13

MAKING THE BEST OF IT

Hendry had a way of resuming a conversation where he had left off the night before. He would revolve a topic in his mind, too, and then begin aloud, "He's a queer ane," or, "Say ye so?" which was at times perplexing. With the whole day before them, none of the family was inclined to waste strength in talk but one morning when he was blowing the steam off his porridge, Hendry said, suddenly—

"He's hame again."

The women-folk gave him time to say to whom he was referring, which he occasionally did as an after-thought. But he began to sup his porridge, making eyes as it went steaming down his throat.

"I dinna ken wha ye mean," Jess said; while Leeby, who was on her knees rubbing the hearthstone a bright blue, paused to catch her father's answer.

"Jeames Geogehan," replied Hendry, with the horn spoon in his mouth.

Leeby turned to Jess for enlightenment.

"Geogehan," repeated Jess; "what, no little Jeames 'at ran awa?"

"Ay, ay, but he's a muckle stoot man noo, an' gey grey."

"Ou, I dinna wonder at that. It's a guid forty year since he ran off."

"I waurant ye couldna say exact hoo lang syne it is?"

Hendry asked this question because Jess was notorious for her memory, and he gloried in putting it to the test.

"Let's see," she said.

"But wha is he?" asked Leeby. "I never kent nae Geogehans in Thrums."

"Weel, it's forty-one years syne come Michaelmas," said Jess.

"Hoo do ye ken?"

"I ken fine. Ye mind his father had been lickin' 'im, an' he ran awa in a passion, cryin' oot 'at he would never come back? Ay, then, he had a pair o' boots on at the time, an' his father ran after 'im an' took them aff 'im. The boots was the last 'at Davie Mearns made, an' it's fully ane-an-forty years since Davie fell ower the quarry on the day o' the hill-market. That settles't. Ay, an' Jeames 'll be turned fifty noo, for he was comin' on for ten year auld at that time. Ay, ay, an' he's come back. What a state Eppie 'll be in!"

"Tell's wha he is, mother."

"Od, he's Eppie Guthrie's son. Her man was William Geogehan, but he died 'afore you was born, an' as Jeames was their only bairn, the name o' Geogehan's been a kind o' lost sicht o'. Hae ye seen him, Hendry? Is't true 'at he made a fortune in thae far-awa countries? Eppie 'll be blawin' aboot him richt?"

"There's nae doubt aboot the siller," said Hendry, "for he drove in a carriage frae Tilliedrum, an' they say he needs a closet to hing his claes in, there's sic a heap o' them. Ay, but that's no a' he's brocht, na, far frae a'."

"Dinna gang awa till ye've telt's a' aboot 'im. What mair has he brocht?"

"He's brocht a wife," said Hendry, twisting his face curiously.

"There's naething surprisin' in that."

"Ay, but there is, though. Ye see, Eppie had a letter frae 'im no mony weeks syne, sayin' 'at he wasna deid, an' he was comin' hame wi' a fortune. He said, too, 'at he was a single man, an' she's been boastin' aboot that, so ye may think 'at she got a surprise when he hands a wuman oot o' the carriage."

"An' no a pleasant ane," said Jess. "Had he been leein'?"

"Na, he was single when he wrote, an' single when he got the length o' Tilliedrum. Ye see, he fell in wi' the lassie there, an' juist gaed clean aff his heid aboot her. After managin' to withstand the women o' foreign lands for a' thae years, he gaed fair skeer aboot this stocky at Tilliedrum. She's juist seventeen year auld an' the auld fule sits wi' his airm round her in Eppie's hoose, though they've been mairit this fortnicht."

"The doited fule," said Jess.

Jeames Geogehan and his bride became the talk of Thrums, and Jess saw them from her window several times. The first time she had only eyes for the jacket with fur round it worn by Mrs. Geogehan, but subsequently she took in Jeames.

"He's tryin' to carry't aff wi' his heid in the air," she said, "but I can see he's fell shamefaced, an' nae wonder. Ay, I sepad he's mair ashamed o't in his heart than she is. It's an awful like thing o' a lassie to marry an auld man. She had dune't for the siller. Ay, there's pounds' worth o' fur aboot that jacket."

"They say she had siller hersel," said Tibbie Birse.

"Dinna tell me," said Jess. "I ken by her wy o' carryin' hersel 'at she never had a jacket like that afore."

Eppie was not the only person in Thrums whom this marriage enraged. Stories had long been alive of Jeames's fortune, which his cousins' children were some day to divide among themselves, and as a consequence these young men and women looked on Mrs. Geogehan as a thief.

"Dinna bring the wife to our hoose, Jeames," one of them told him, "for we would be fair ashamed to hae her. We used to hae a respect for yer name, so we couldna look her i' the face."

"She's mair like yer dochter than yer wife," said another.

"Na," said a third, "naebody could mistak her for yer dochter. She's ower young-like for that."

"Wi' the siller you'll leave her, Jeames," Tammas Haggart told him, "she'll get a younger man for her second venture."

All this was very trying to the newly-married man, who was thirsting for sympathy. Hendry was the person whom he took into his confidence.

"It may hae been foolish at my time o' life," Hendry reported him to have said, "but I couldnae help it. If they juist kent her better they couldnae but see 'at she's a terrible takkin' crittur."

Jeames was generous; indeed he had come home with the

intention of scattering largess. A beggar met him one day on the brae, and got a shilling from him. She was waving her arms triumphantly as she passed Hendry's house, and Leeby got the story from her.

"Eh, he's a fine man tha, an' a saft ane," the woman said. "I juist speired at 'im hoo his bonny wife was, an' he oot wi' a shillin'!"

Leeby did not keep this news to herself, and soon it was through the town. Jeames's face began to brighten.

"They're comin' round to a mair sensible wy o' lookin' at things," he told Hendry. "I was walkin' wi' the wife i' the buryin' ground yesterday, an' we met Kitty McQueen. She was ane o' the warst agin me at first, but she telt me i' the buryin' ground 'at when a man mairit he should please 'imsel. Oh, they're comin' round."

What Kitty told Jess was—

"I minded o' the tinkler wuman 'at he gae a shillin' to, so I thocht I would butter up at the auld fule too. Weel, I assure ye, I had nae suner said 'at he was rale wise to marry wha he likit than he slips a pound note into my hand. Ou, Jess, we've taen the wrang wy wi' Jeames. I've telt a' my bairns 'at if they meet him they're to praise the wife terrible, an' I'm far mista'en if that doesna mean five shillins to ilka ane o' them."

Jean Whamond got a pound note for saying that Jeames's wife had an uncommon pretty voice, and Davit Lunan had ten shillings for a judicious word about her attractive manners. Tibbie Birse invited the newly-married couple to tea (one pound).

"They're takkin' to her, they're takkin' to her," Jeames said, gleefully. "I kent they would come round in time. Ay, even my mother, 'at was sae mad at first, sits for hours noo aside her, haudin' her hand. They're juist inseparable."

The time came when we had Mr. and Mrs. Geogehan and Eppie to tea.

"It's true enough," Leeby ran ben to tell Jess, " 'at Eppie an' the wife's fond o' ane another. I wouldna hae believed it o' Eppie if I hadna seen it, but I assure ye they sat even at the tea-table haudin' ane another's hands. I waurant they're doin't this meenute."

"I wasna born on a Sabbath," retorted Jess. "Na, na, dinna tell me Eppie's fond o' her. Tell Eppie to come but to the kitchen when the tea's ower."

Jess and Eppie had half an hour's conversation alone, and then our guests left.

"It's a richt guid thing," said Hendry, " 'at Eppie has ta'en sic a notion o' the wife."

"Ou, ay," said Jess.

Then Hendry hobbled out of the house.

"What said Eppie to ye?" Leeby asked her mother.

"Juist what I expeckit," Jess answered. "Ye see she's dependent on Jeames, so she has to butter up at 'im."

"Did she say onything aboot haudin' the wife's hand sae fond-like?"

"Ay, she said it was an awfu' trial to her, an' 'at it sickened her to see Jeames an' the wife baith believin' 'at she likit to do't."

Chapter 14

VISITORS AT THE MANSE

On bringing home his bride, the minister showed her to us, and we thought she would do when she realized that she was not the minister. She was a grand lady from Edinburgh, though very frank, and we simple folk amused her a good deal, especially when we were sitting cowed in the manse parlour drinking a dish of tea with her, as happened to Leeby, her father, and me, three days before Jamie came home.

Leeby had refused to be drawn into conversation, like one who knew her place, yet all her actions were genteel and her monosyllabic replies in the Englishy tongue, as of one who was, after all, a little above the common. When the minister's wife asked her whether she took sugar and cream, she said politely, "If you please" (though she did not take sugar), a reply that contrasted with Hendry's equally well-intended answer to the same question. "I'm no partikler," was what Hendry said.

Hendry had left home glumly, declaring that the white collar Jess had put on him would throttle him; but her feikieness ended in his surrender, and he was looking unusually perjink. Had not his daughter been present he would have been the most at ease of the company, but her manners were too fine not to make an impression upon one who knew her on her everyday behaviour, and she had also ways of bringing Hendry to himself by a touch beneath the table. It was in church that Leeby brought to perfection her manner of looking after her father. When he had confidence in the preacher's soundness, he would sometimes have slept in his pew if Leeby had not had a watchful foot. She wakened him in an instant, while still looking modestly at the pulpit; however reverently he might try to fall over, Leeby's foot went out. She was such an artist that I never caught her in the act. All I knew for certain was that, now and then, Hendry suddenly sat up.

The ordeal was over when Leeby went upstairs to put on her things. After tea Hendry had become bolder in talk, his subject being ministerial. He had an extraordinary knowledge, got no one knew where, of the matrimonial affairs of all the ministers in these parts, and his stories about them ended frequently with a chuckle. He always took it for granted that a minister's marriage was womanhood's great triumph, and that the particular woman who got him must be very clever. Some of his tales were even more curious than he thought them, such as the one Leeby tried to interrupt by saying we must be going.

"There's Mr. Pennycuick, noo," said Hendry, shaking his head in wonder at what he had to tell; "him 'at's minister at Tilliedrum. Weel, when he was a probationer he was michty poor, an' one day he was walkin' into Thrums frae Glen Quharity, an' he tak's a rest at a little housey on the road. The fowk didna ken him ava, but they saw he was a minister, an' the lassie was sorry to see him wi' sic an auld hat. What think ye she did?"

"Come away, father," said Leeby, re-entering the parlour; but Hendry was now in full pursuit of his story.

"I'll tell ye what she did," he continued. "She juist took his hat awa, an' put her father's new ane in its place, an' Mr. Pennycuick never kent the differ till he landed in Thrums. It was terrible kind o' her. Ay, but the auld man would be in a michty rage when he found she had swappit the hats."

"Come away," said Leeby, still politely, though she was burning to tell her mother how Hendry had disgraced them.

"The minister," said Hendry, turning his back on Leeby, "didna forget the lassie. Na; as sune as he got a kirk, he married her. Ay, she got her reward. He married her. It was rale noble o' 'im."

I do not know what Leeby said to Hendry when she got him beyond the manse gate, for I stayed behind to talk to the minister. As it turned out, the minister's wife did most of the talking, smiling good-humouredly at country gawkiness the while.

"Yes," she said, "I am sure I shall like Thrums, though those teas to the congregation are a little trying. Do you know, Thrums is the only place I was ever in where it struck me that the men are cleverer than the women."

She told us why.

"Well, to-night affords a case in point. Mr. McQumpha was quite brilliant, was he not, in comparison with his daughter? Really, she seemed so put out at being at the manse that she could not raise her eyes. I question if she would know me again, and I am sure she sat in the room as one blindfolded. I left her in the bedroom a minute, and I assure you, when I returned she was still standing on the same spot in the centre of the floor."

I pointed out that Leeby had been awestruck.

"I suppose so," she said; "but it is a pity she cannot make use of her eyes, if not of her tongue. Ah, the Thrums women are good, I believe, but their wits are sadly in need of sharpening. I daresay it comes of living in so small a place."

I overtook Leeby on the brae, aware, as I saw her alone, that it had been her father whom I passed talking to Tammas Haggart in the Square. Hendry stopped to have what he called a tove with any likely person he encountered, and, indeed, though he and I often took a walk on Saturdays, I generally lost him before we were clear of the town.

In a few moments Leeby and I were at home to give Jess the news.

"Whaur's yer father?" asked Jess, as if Hendry's way of dropping behind was still unknown to her.

"Ou, I left him speakin' to Gavin Birse," said Leeby. "I daursay he's awa to some hoose."

"It's no very silvendy (safe) his comin' ower the brae by himsel," said Jess, adding in a bitter tone of conviction, "but he'll gang in to no hoose as lang as he's so weel dressed. Na, he would think it boastfu'."

I sat down to a book by the kitchen fire; but, as Leeby became communicative, I read less and less. While she spoke she was baking bannocks with all the might of her, and Jess, leaning forward in her chair, was arranging them in a semicircle round the fire.

"Na," was the first remark of Leeby's that came between me and my book, "it is no new furniture."

"But there was three cart-loads o't, Leeby, sent on frae Edinbory. Tibbie Birse helpit to lift it in and she said the parlour furniture beat a'."

"Ou, it's substantial, but it is no new. I sepad it had been bocht cheap second-hand, for the chair I had was terrible scratched like, an', what's mair, the armchair was a heap shinnier than the rest."

"Ay, ay, I wager it had been new stuffed. Tibbie said the carpet cowed for grandeur!"

"Oh, I dinna deny it's a guid carpet; but if it's been turned once it's been turned half a dozen times, so it's far frae new. Ay, an' forby, it was rale threadbare aneath the table, so ye may be sure they've been cuttin't an' puttin' the worn pairt whaur it would be least seen."

"They say 'at there's twa grand gas brackets i' the parlour, an' a wonderfu' gasoliery i' the dinin'-room?"

"We wasna i' the dinin'-room, so I ken naething aboot the gasoliery; but I'll tell ye what the gas brackets is. I recognized them immeditly. Ye mind the auld gasoliery i' the dinin'-room had twa lichts? Ay, then, the parlour brackets is made oot o' the auld gasoliery."

"Weel, Leeby, as sure as ye're standin' there, that passed through my head as sune as Tibbie mentioned them!"

"There's nae doot about it. Ay, I was in ane o' the bedrooms, too!"

"It would be grand?"

"I wouldna say 'at it was partikler grand, but there was a great mask (quantity) o' things in't, an' near everything was covered wi' cretonne. But the chairs dinna match. There was a very bonny-painted cloth alang the chimley — what they call a mantelpiece border, I warrant."

"Sal, I've often wondered what they was."

"Weel, I assure ye they winna be ill to mak, for the border was juist nailed upon a board laid on the chimley. There's naething to hender's makin' ane for the room."

"Ay, we could sew something on the border instead o' paintin't. The room lookit weel, ye say?"

"Yes, but it was economically furnished. There was nae carpet below the wax-cloth; na, there was nane below the bed either."

"Was't a grand bed?"

"It had a fell lot o' brass aboot it, but there was juist one pair o' blankets. I thocht it was gey shabby, hae'n the ewer a different pattern frae the basin; ay, an' there was juist a poker in the fireplace, there was nae tangs."

"Yea, yea; they'll hae but one set o' bedroom fire-irons. The tangs 'll be in anither room. Tod, that's no sae michty grand for Edinbory. What like was she hersel?"

"Ou, very ladylike and saft spoken. She's a canty body an' frank. She wears her hair low on the left side to hod (hide) a scar, an' there's twa warts on her richt hand."

"There hadna been a fire i' the parlour?"

"No, but it was ready to licht. There was sticks and paper in't. The paper was oot o' a dressmaker's journal."

"Ye say so? She'll mak her ain frocks, I sepad."

When Hendry entered to take off his collar and coat before sitting down to his evening meal of hot water, porter, and bread mixed in a bowl, Jess sent me off to the attic. As I climbed the stairs I remembered that the minister's wife thought Leeby in need of sharpening.

Chapter 15

HOW GAVIN BIRSE PUT IT TO MAG LOWNIE

In a wet day the rain gathered in blobs on the road that passed our garden. Then it crawled into the cart-tracks until the road was streaked with water. Lastly, the water gathered in heavy yellow pools. If the on-ding still continued, clods of earth toppled from the garden dyke into the ditch.

On such a day, when even the dulseman had gone into shelter, and the women scudded by with their wrappers over their heads, came Gavin Birse to our door. Gavin, who was the Glen Quharity post, was still young, but had never been quite the same man since some amateurs in the glen ironed his back for rheumatism. I thought he had called to have a crack with me. He sent his compliments up to the attic, however, by Leeby, and would I come and be a witness?

Gavin came up and explained. He had taken off his scarf and thrust it into his pocket, lest the rain should take the colour out of it. His boots cheeped, and his shoulders had risen to his ears. He stood steaming before my fire.

"If it's no' ower muckle to ask ye," he said, "I would like ye for a witness."

"A witness! But for what do you need a witness, Gavin?"

"I want ye," he said, "to come wi' me to Mag's, and be a witness."

Gavin and Mag Birse had been engaged for a year or more. Mag was the daughter of Janet Ogilvy, who was best remembered as the body that took the hill (that is, wandered about it) for twelve hours on the day Mr. Dishart, the Auld Licht minister, accepted a call to another church.

"You don't mean to tell me, Gavin," I, asked, "that your marriage is to take place to-day?"

By the twist of his mouth I saw that he was only deferring a smile.

"Far frae that," he said.

"Ah, then, you have quarrelled, and I am to speak up for you?"

"Na, na," he said, " I dinna want ye to do that above all things. It would be a favour if ye could gie me a bad character."

This beat me, and, I daresay, my face showed it.

"I'm no' juist what ye would call anxious to marry Mag noo," said Gavin, without a tremor.

I told him to go on.

"There's a lassie oot at Craigiebuckle," he explained, "workin' on the farm—Jeanie Luke by name. Ye may hae seen her?"

"What of her?" I asked, severely.

"Weel," said Gavin, still unabashed, "I'm thinkin' noo 'at I would rather hae her."

Then he stated his case more fully.

"Ay, I thocht I liked Mag oncommon till I saw Jeanie, an' I like her fine yet, but I prefer the other ane. That state o' matters canna gang on for ever, so I came into Thrums the day to settle't one wy or another."

"And how," I asked, "do you propose going about it? It is a somewhat delicate business."

"Ou, I see nae great difficulty in't. I'll speir at Mag, blunt oot, if she'll let me aff. Yes, I'll put it to her plain."

"You're sure Jeanie would take you?"

"Ay; oh, there's nae fear o' that."

"But if Mag keeps you to your bargain?"

"Weel, in that case there's nae harm done."

"You are in a great hurry, Gavin?"

"Ye may say that; but I want to be married. The wifie I lodge wi' canna last lang, an' I would like to settle doon in some place."

"So you are on your way to Mag's now?"

"Ay, we'll get her in atween twal' and ane."

"Oh, yes; but why do you want me to go with you?"

"I want ye for a witness. If she winna let me aff, weel and guid; and if she will, it's better to hae a witness in case she should go back on her word."

Gavin made his proposal briskly, and as coolly as if he were only asking me to go fishing; but I did not accompany him to Mag's. He left, the house to look for another witness, and about an hour afterwards Jess saw him pass with Tammas Haggart. Tammas cried in during the evening to tell us how the mission prospered.

"Mind ye," said Tammas, a drop of water hanging to the point of his nose, "I disclaim all responsibility in the business. I ken Mag weel for a thrifty, respectable woman, as her mither was afore her, and so I said to Gavin when he came to speir me."

"Ay, mony a pirn has 'Lisbeth filled to me," said Hendry, settling down to a reminiscence.

"No to be ower hard on Gavin," continued Tammas, forestalling Hendry, "he took what I said in guid part; but aye when I stopped speakin' to draw breath, he says, 'The queistion is, will ye come wi' me?' He was michty made up in 's mind."

"Weel, ye went wi' him," suggested Jess, who wanted to bring Tammas to the point.

"Ay," said the stone-breaker," but no in sic a hurry as that."

He worked his mouth round and round, to clear the course, as it were, for a sarcasm.

"Fowk often say," he continued, " 'at 'am quick beyond the ordinar' in seein' the humorous side o' things."

Here Tammas paused, and looked at us.

"So ye are, Tammas," said Hendry. "Losh, ye mind hoo ye saw the humorous side o' me wearin' a pair o' boots 'at wisna marrows! No, the ane had a toe-piece on, an' the other hadna."

"Ye juist wore them sometimes when ye was delvin'," broke in Jess, "ye have as guid a pair o' boots as ony in Thrums."

"Ay, but I had worn them," said Hendry, "at odd times for mair than a year, an' I had never seen the humorous side o' them. Weel, as fac as death (here he addressed me), Tammas had juist seen them twa or three times when he saw the humorous side o' them. Syne I saw their humorous side, too, but no till Tammas pointed it oot."

"That was naething," said Tammas, "naething ava to some things I've done."

"But what aboot Mag?" said Leeby.

"We wasna that length, was we?" said Tammas. "Na, we was speakin' aboot the humorous side. Ay, wait a wee, I didna mention the humorous side for naething."

He paused to reflect.

"Oh, yes," he said at last, brightening up, "I was sayin' to ye hoo quick I was to see the humorous side o' onything. Ay, then, what made me say that was 'at in a clink (flash) I saw the humorous side o' Gavin's position."

"Man, man," said Hendry, admiringly, "and what is't?"

"Oh, it's this, there's something humorous in speirin' a woman to let ye aff so as ye can be married to another woman."

"I daursay there is," said Hendry, doubtfully.

"Did she let him aff?" asked Jess, taking the words out of Leeby's mouth.

"I'm comin' to that," said Tammas. "Gavin proposes to me after I had haen my laugh— "

"Yes," cried Hendry, banging the table with his fist, "it has a humorous side. Ye're richt again, Tammas."

"I wish ye wadna blatter (beat) the table," said Jess, and then Tammas proceeded.

"Gavin wanted me to tak paper an' ink an' a pen wi' me, to write the proceedins doon, but I said, 'Na, na, I'll tak paper, but no nae ink nor nae pen, for there'll be ink an' a pen there.' That was what I said."

"An' did she let him aff?" asked Leeby.

"Weel" said Tammas, "aff we goes to Mag's hoose, an' sure enough Mag was in. She was alane, too; so Gavin, no to waste time, juist sat doon for politeness' sake, an' syne rises up again; an' says he, 'Marget Lownie, I hae a solemn question to speir at ye, namely this, Will you, Marget Lownie, let me, Gavin Birse, aff?' "

"Mag would start at that?"

"Sal, she was braw an' cool. I thocht she maun hae got wind o' his intentions aforehand, for she juist replies, quiet-like, 'Hoo do ye want aff, Gavin?'

" 'Because,' says he, like a book, 'my affections has undergone a change.'

" 'Ye mean Jean Luke,' says Mag.

" 'That is wha I mean,' says Gavin, very straitforrard."

"But she didna let him aff, did she?"

"Na, she wasna the kind. Says she, 'I wonder to hear ye, Gavin, but 'am no goin' to agree to naething o' that sort.'

" 'Think it ower,' says Gavin.

" 'Na, my mind's made up,' said she.

" 'Ye would sune get anither man,' he says, earnestly.

" 'Hoo do I ken that?' she speirs, rale sensibly, I thocht, for men's no sae easy to get.

" 'Am sure o't,' Gavin says, wi' michty conviction in his voice, 'for ye're bonny to look at, an' weel-kent for bein' a guid body.'

" 'Ay,' says Mag, 'I'm glad ye like me, Gavin, for ye have to tak me.'"

"That put a clincher on him," interrupted Hendry.

"He was loth to gie in," replied Tammas, "so he says, 'Ye think 'am a fine character, Marget Lownie, but ye're very far mista'en. I wouldna wonder but what I was lossin' my place some o' thae days, an' syne whaur would ye be? — Marget Lownie,' he goes on, ' 'am nat'rally lazy an' fond o' the drink. As sure as ye stand there, 'am a reglar devil!'"

"That was strong language," said Hendry, "but he would be wantin' to fleg (frighten) her?"

"Juist so, but he didna manage't, for Mag says, 'We a' hae oor faults, Gavin, an' deevil or no deevil, ye're the man for me!'

"Gavin thocht a bit," continued Tammas, "an' syne he tries her on a new tack. 'Marget Lownie,' he says, 'ye're father's an auld man noo, an' he has naebody but yersel to look after him. I'm thinkin' it would be kind o' cruel o' me to tak ye awa frae him?'"

"Mag wouldna be ta'en in wi' that; she wasna born on a Sawbath," said Jess, using one of her favourite sayings.

"She wasna," answered Tammas. "Says she, 'Hae nae fear on that score, Gavin my father's fine willin' to spare me!'"

"An' that ended it?"

"Ay, that ended it."

"Did ye tak it doon in writin'?" asked Hendry.

"There was nae need," said Tammas, handing round his snuff-mull. "No, I never touched paper. When I saw the thing was settled, I left them to their coortin'. They're to tak a look at Snecky Hobart's auld hoose the nicht. It's to let."

Chapter 16

THE SON FROM LONDON

In the spring of the year there used to come to Thrums a painter from nature whom Hendry spoke of as the drawer. He lodged with Jess in my attic, and when the weavers met him they said, "Weel, drawer," and then passed on, grinning. Tammas Haggart was the first to say this.

The drawer was held a poor man because he straggled about the country looking for subjects for his draws, and Jess, as was her way, gave him many comforts for which she would not charge. That, I daresay, was why he painted for her a little portrait of Jamie. When the drawer came back to Thrums he always found the painting in a frame in the room. Here I must make a confession about Jess. She did not in her secret mind think the portrait quite the thing, and as soon as the drawer departed it was removed from the frame to make way for a calendar. The deception was very innocent, Jess being anxious not to hurt the donor's feelings.

To those who have the artist's eye, the picture, which hangs in my school-house now, does not show a handsome lad, Jamie being short and dapper, with straw-coloured hair, and a chin that ran away into his neck. That is how I once regarded him, but I have little heart for criticism of those I like, and, despite his madness for a season, of which, alas, I shall have to tell, I am always Jamie's friend. Even to hear any one disparaging the appearance of Jess's son is to me a pain.

All Jess's acquaintances knew that in the beginning of every month a registered letter reached her from London. To her it was not a matter to keep secret. She was proud that the help she and Hendry needed in the gloaming of their lives should come from her beloved son, and the neighbours esteemed Jamie because he was good to his mother. Jess had more humour than any other woman I have known, while Leeby was but sparingly endowed; yet, as the month neared its close, it was the daughter who put on the humorist, Jess thinking money too serious a thing to jest about. Then if Leeby had a moment for gossip, as when ironing a dickey for Hendry, and the iron was a trifle too hot, she would look archly at me before addressing her mother in these words:

"Will he send, think ye?"

Jess, who had a conviction that he would send, affected surprise at the question.

"Will Jamie send this month, do ye mean? Na, oh, losh no! it's no, to be expeckit. Na, he couldna do't this time."

"That's what ye aye say, but he aye sends. Yes, an' vara weel ye ken 'at he will send."

"Na, na, Leeby; dinna let me ever think o' sic a thing this month."

"As if ye wasna thinkin' o't day an' nicht!"

"He's terrible mindfu', Leeby, but he doesna hae't. Na, no this month; mebbe next month."

"Do you mean to tell me, mother, 'at ye'll no be up oot o' yer bed on Monunday an hour afore yer usual time, lookin' for the post?"

"Na, no this time. I may be up, an' tak a look for 'im, but no expeckin' a registerdy; na, na, that wouldna be reasonable."

"Reasonable here, reasonable there, up you'll be, keekin' (peering) through the blind to see if the post's comin', ay, an' what's mair, the post will come, and a registerdy in his hand wi' fifteen shillings in't at the least."

"Dinna say fifteen, Leeby; I would never think o' sic a sum. Mebbe five—"

"Five! I wonder to hear ye. Vera weel you ken 'at since he had twenty-twa shillings in the week he's never sent less than half a sovereign."

"No, but we canna expeck—"

"Expeck! No, but it's no expeck, it's get."

On the Monday morning when I came downstairs, Jess was in

her chair by the window, beaming, a piece of paper in her hand. I did not require to be told about it, but I was told. Jess had been up before Leeby could get the fire lit, with great difficulty reaching the window in her bare feet, and many a time had she said that the post must be by.

"Havers," said Leeby, "he winna be for an hour yet. Come awa' back to your bed."

"Na, he maun be by," Jess would say in a few minutes; "ou, we couldna expeck this month."

So it went on until Jess's hand shook the blind.

"He's comin', Leeby, he's comin'. He'll no hae naething, na, I couldna expeck — He's by!"

"I dinna believe it," cried Leeby, running to the window, "he's juist at his tricks again."

This was in reference to a way our saturnine post had of pretending that he brought no letters and passing the door. Then he turned back. "Mistress McQumpha," he cried, and whistled.

"Run, Leeby, run," said Jess, excitedly.

Leeby hastened to the door, and came back with a registered letter.

"Registerdy," she cried in triumph, and Jess, with fond hands, opened the letter. By the time I came down the money was hid away in a box beneath the bed, where not even Leeby could find it, and Jess was on her chair hugging the letter. She preserved all her registered envelopes.

This was the first time I had been in Thrums when Jamie was expected for his ten days' holiday, and for a week we discussed little else. Though he had written saying when he would sail for Dundee, there was quite a possibility of his appearing on the brae at any moment, for he liked to take Jess and Leeby by surprise. Hendry there was no surprising, unless he was in the mood for it, and the coolness of him was one of Jess's grievances. Just two years earlier Jamie came north a week before his time, and his father saw him from the window. Instead of crying out in amazement or

hacking his face, for he was shaving at the time, Hendry calmly
wiped his razor on the window-sill, and said—

"Ay there's Jamie."

Jamie was a little disappointed at being seen in this way, for he
had been looking forward for four and forty hours to repeating the
sensation of the year before. On that occasion he had got to the
door unnoticed, where he stopped to listen. I daresay he checked
his breath, the better to catch his mother's voice, for Jess being an
invalid, Jamie thought of her first. He had Leeby sworn to write
the truth about her, but many an anxious hour he had on hearing
that she was "complaining fell (considerably) about her back the
day," Leeby, as he knew, being frightened to alarm him. Jamie, too,
had given his promise to tell exactly how he was keeping, but often
he wrote that he was "fine" when Jess had her doubts. When
Hendry wrote he spread himself over the table, and said that Jess
was "juist about it", or "aff and on," which does not tell much. So
Jamie hearkened painfully at the door, and by and by heard his
mother say to Leeby that she was sure the teapot was running out.
Perhaps that voice was as sweet to him as the music of a maiden to
her lover, but Jamie did not rush into his mother's arms. Jess had
told me with a beaming face how craftily he behaved. The old man,
of lungs that shook Thrums by night, who went from door to door
selling firewood, had a way of shoving doors rudely open and crying—

"Ony rozetty roots?" and him Jamie imitated.

"Juist think," Jess said, as she recalled the incident, "what a
startle we got. As we think, Pete kicks open the door and cries oot,
'Ony rozetty roots?' and Leeby says 'No', and gangs to shut the door.
Next minute she screeches, 'What, what, what!' and in walks
Jamie!"

Jess was never able to decide whether it was more delightful to
be taken aback in this way or to prepare for Jamie. Sudden
excitement was bad for her according to Hendry, who got his
medical knowledge second-hand from persons under treatment,
but with Jamie's appearance on the threshold Jess's health began

to improve. This time he kept to the appointed day, and the house was turned upside down in his honour. Such a polish did Leeby put on the flagons which hung on the kitchen wall, that, passing between them and the window, I thought once I had been struck by lightning. On the morning of the day that was to bring him, Leeby was up at two o'clock, and eight hours before, he could possibly arrive Jess had a night-shirt warming for him at the fire. I was no longer anybody, except as a person who could give Jamie advice. Jess told me what I was to say. The only thing he and his mother quarrelled about was the underclothing she would swaddle him in, and Jess asked me to back her up in her entreaties.

"There's no a doubt," she said, "but what it's a hantle caulder here than in London, an' it would be a terrible business if he was to tak the cauld."

Jamie was to sail from London to Dundee, and come on to Thrums from Tilliedrum in the post-cart. The road at that time, however, avoided thebrae, and at a certain point Jamie's custom was to alight, and take the short cut home, along a farm road and up the commonty. Here, too, Hookey Crewe, the post, deposited his passenger's box, which Hendry wheeled home in a barrow. Long before the cart had lost sight of Tilliedrum, Jess was at her window.

"Tell her Hookey's often late on Monundays," Leeby whispered to me, "for she'll gang oot o' her mind if she thinks there's onything wrang."

Soon Jess was painfully excited, though she sat as still as salt.

"It maun be yer time," she said, looking at both Leeby and me, for in Thrums we went out and met our friends.

"Hoots," retorted Leeby, trying to be hardy, "Hookey canna be oot o' Tilliedrum yet."

"He maun hae startit lang syne."

"I wonder at ye, mother, puttin' yersel in sic a state. Ye'll he ill when he comes."

"Na, 'am no in nae state, Leeby, but there'll no be nae accident, will there?"

"It's most provokin' 'at ye will think 'at every time Jamie steps into a machine there'll be an accident. 'Am sure if ye would tak mair after my father, it would be a blessin'. Look hoo cool he is."

"Whaur is he, Leeby?"

"Oh, I dinna ken. The henmost time I saw him he was layin' doon the law aboot something to T'nowhead."

"It's an awfu' wy that, he has o' ga'en oot withoot a word. I wouldna wonder 'at he's no bein' in time to meet Jamie, an' that would be a pretty business."

"Od, ye're sure he'll be in braw time."

"But he hasna ta'en the barrow wi' him, an' hoo is Jamie's luggage to be brocht up withoot a barrow?"

"Barrow! He took the barrow to the saw-mill an hour syne to pick it up at Rob Angus's on the wy."

Several times Jess was sure she saw the cart in the distance, and implored us to be off.

"I'll tak no settle till ye're awa," she said, her face now flushed and her hands working nervously.

"We've time to gang and come twa or three times yet," remonstrated Leeby; but Jess gave me so beseeching a look that I put on my hat. Then Hendry dandered in to change his coat deliberately, and when the three of us set off, we left Jess with her eye on the door by which Jamie must enter. He was her only son now, and she had not seen him for a year.

On the way down the commonty, Leeby had the honour of being twice addressed as Miss McQumpha, but her father was Hendry to all, which shows that we make our social position for ourselves. Hendry looked forward to Jamie's annual appearance only a little less hungrily than Jess, but his pulse still beat regularly. Leeby would have considered it almost wicked to talk of anything except Jamie now, but Hendry cried out comments on the tatties, yesterday's roup, the fall in jute, to everybody he encountered. When he and a crony had their say and parted, it was their custom to continue the conversation in shouts until they were out of hearing.

Only to Jess at her window was the cart late that afternoon. Jamie jumped from it in the long great-coat that had been new to Thrums the year before, and Hendry said calmly —

"Ay, Jamie."

Leeby and Jamie made signs that they recognized each other as brother and sister, but I was the only one with whom he shook hands. He was smart in his movements and quite the gentleman, but the Thrums ways took hold of him again at once. He even inquired for his mother in a tone that was meant to deceive me into thinking he did not care how she was.

Hendry would have had a talk out of him on the spot, but was reminded of the luggage. We took the heavy farm road, and soon we were at the saw-mill. I am naturally leisurely, but we climbed the commonty at a stride. Jamie pretended to be calm, but in a dark place I saw him take Leeby's hand, and after that he said not a word. His eyes were fixed an the elbow of the brae, where, he would come into sight of his mother's window. Many, many a time, I know, that lad had prayed to God for still another sight of the window with his mother at it. So we came to the corner where the stile is that Sam'l Dickie jumped in the race for T'nowhead's Bell, and before Jamie was the house of his childhood and his mother's window, and the fond, anxious face of his mother herself. My eyes are dull, and I did not see her, but suddenly Jamie cried out, "My mother!" and Leeby and I were left behind. When I reached the kitchen Jess was crying, and her son's arms were round her neck. I went away to my attic.

There was only one other memorable event of that day. Jamie had finished his tea, and we all sat round him, listening to his adventures and opinions. He told us how the country should be governed, too, and perhaps put on airs a little. Hendry asked the questions, and Jamie answered them as pat as if he and his father were going through the Shorter Catechism. When Jamie told anything marvellous, as how many towels were used at the shop in a day, or that twopence was the charge for a single shave, his father screwed his mouth together as if preparing to whistle, and then instead made a curious clucking noise with his tongue, which was reserved for the expression of absolute amazement. As for Jess, who was given to making much of me, she ignored my remarks, and laughed hilariously at jokes of Jamie's which had been received in silence from me a few minutes before.

Slowly it came to me that Leeby had something on her mind, and that Jamie was talking to her with his eyes. I learned afterwards that they were plotting how to get me out of the kitchen, but were too impatient to wait. Thus it was that the great event happened in my presence. Jamie rose and stood near Jess — I daresay he had planned the scene frequently. Then he produced from his pocket a purse, and coolly opened it. Silence fell upon us as we saw that purse. From it he took a neatly-folded piece of paper, crumpled it into a ball, and flung it into Jess's lap.

I cannot say whether Jess knew what it was. Her hand shook, and for a moment she let the ball of paper lie there.

"Open't up," cried Leeby, who was in the secret.

"What is't ?" asked Hendry, drawing nearer.

"It's juist a bit paper Jamie flung at me," said Jess, and then she unfolded it.

"It's a five-pound note!" cried Hendry.

"Na, na; oh keep us, no," said Jess; but she knew it was.

For a time she could not speak.

"I canna tak it, Jamie," she faltered at last.

But Jamie waved his hand, meaning that it was nothing, and then, lest he should burst, hurried out into the garden, where he walked up and down whistling. May God bless the lad, thought I. I do not know the history of that five-pound note, but well aware I am that it grew slowly out of pence and silver, and that Jamie denied his passions many things for this great hour. His sacrifices watered his young heart and kept it fresh and tender. Let us no longer cheat our consciences by talking of filthy lucre. Money may always be a beautiful thing. It is we who make it grimy.

Chapter 17

A HOME FOR GENIUSES

From hints he had let drop at odd times I knew that Tammas Haggart had a scheme for geniuses, but not until the evening after Jamie's arrival did I get it out of him. Hendry was with Jamie at the fishing, and it came about that Tammas and I had the pig-sty to ourselves.

"Of course," he said, when we had got a grip of the subject, "I dount pretend as my ideas is to be followed withoot deeviation, but ondootedly something should be done for geniuses, them bein' aboot the only class as we do naething for. Yet they're fowk to be prood o', an' we shouldna let them overdo the thing, nor run into debt; na, na. There was Robbie Burns, noo, as real a genius as ever—"

At the pig-sty, where we liked to have more than one topic, we had frequently to tempt Tammas away from Burns.

"Your scheme," I interposed, "is for living geniuses, of course?"

"Ay," he said, thoughtfully, "them 'at's gone canna be brocht back. Weel, my idea is 'at a Home should be built for geniuses at the public expense, whaur they could all live thegither, an' be decently looked after. Na, no in London; that's no my plan, but I would hae't within an hour's distance o' London, say five mile frae the market-place, an' standin' in a bit garden, whaur the geniuses could walk aboot arm-in-arm, composin' their minds."

"You would have the grounds walled in, I suppose, so that the public could not intrude?"

"Weel, there's a difficulty there, because, ye'll observe, as the public would support the institootion, they would hae a kind o' richt to look in. How-some-ever, I daur say we could arrange to fling the grounds open to the public once a week on condition 'at they didna speak to the geniuses. I'm thinkin' 'at if there was a small chairge for admission the Home could be made self-supportin'. Losh! to think 'at if there had been sic an institootion in his time a man micht hae sat on the bit dyke and watched Robbie Burns danderin' roond the—"

"You would divide the Home into suites of rooms, so that every inmate would have his own apartments?"

"Not by no means; na, na. The mair I read aboot geniuses the mair clearly I see as their wy o' living alane ower muckle is ane o' the things as, breaks doon their health, and makes them meeserable. I' the Home they would hae a bedroom apiece, but the parlour an' the other sittin'-rooms would be for all, so as they could enjoy ane another's company. The management? Oh, that's aisy. The superintendent would be a medical man appointed by Parliament, and he would hae men-servants to do his biddin'."

"Not all men-servants, surely?"

"Every one o' them. Man, geniuses is no to be trusted wi' womenfolk. No, even Robbie Bu—"

"So he did; but would the inmates have to put themselves entirely in the superintendent's hands?"

"Nae doubt; an' they would see it was the wisest thing they could do. He would be careful o' their health, an' send them early to bed as weel as hae them up at eight sharp. Geniuses' healths is always breakin' doon because of late hours, as in the case o' the lad wha used often to begin his immortal writin's at twal' o'clock at nicht, a thing 'at would ruin ony constitootion. But the superintendent would see as they had a tasty supper at nine o'clock—something as agreed wi' them. Then for half an hour they would quiet their brains readin' oot aloud, time about, frae sic a book as the *Pilgrim's Progress*, an' the gas would be turned aff at ten precisely."

"When would you have them up in the morning?"

"At sax in summer an' seven in winter. The superintendent would see as they were all properly bathed every mornin', cleanliness bein' most important for the preservation o' health."

"This sounds well; but suppose a genius broke the rules—lay in bed, for instance, reading by the light of a candle after hours, or refused to take his bath in the morning?"

"The superintendent would hae to punish him. The genius would be sent back to his bed, maybe. An' if he lay lang i' the mornin' he would hae to gang withoot his breakfast."

"That would be all very well where the inmate only broke the regulations once in a way; but suppose he were to refuse to take his bath day after day (and, you know, geniuses are said to be eccentric in that particular), what would be done? You could not starve him; geniuses are too scarce."

"Na, na; in a case like that he would hae to be reported to the public. The thing would hae to come afore the Hoose o' Commons. Ay, the superintendent would get a member o' the Opposeetion to ask a queistion such as 'Can the honourable gentleman, the Secretary of State for Home Affairs, inform the Hoose whether it is a fac that Mr. Sic-a-one, the well-known genius, at present resident in the Home for Geniuses, has, contrairy to regulations, perseestently and obstinately refused to change his linen; and, if so, whether the Government proposes to take ony steps in the matter?' The newspapers would report the discussion next mornin', an' so it would be made public withoot onnecessary ootlay."

"In a general way, however, you would give the geniuses perfect freedom? They could work when they liked, and come and go when they liked?"

"Not so. The superintendent would fix the hours o' wark, an' they would all write, or whatever it was, thegither in one large room. Man, man, it would mak a grand draw for a painter-chield, that room, wi' all the geniuses working awa' thegither."

"But when the labours of the day were over the genius would be at liberty to make calls by himself, or to run up, say, to London for an hour or two?"

"Hoots no, that would spoil everything. It's the drink, ye see, as does for a terrible lot o' geniuses. Even Rob—"

"Alas! yes. But would you have them all teetotalers?"

"What do ye tak me for? Na, na; the superintendent would allow them one glass o' toddy every nicht, an' mix it himsel; but he would never let the keys o' the press, whaur he kept the drink, oot o' his hands. They would never be allowed oot o' the gairden either, withoot a man to look after them; an' I wouldna burthen them wi' ower muckle pocket-money. Saxpence in the week would be suffeecient."

"How about their clothes?"

"They would get twa suits a year, wi' the letter G sewed on the shoulders, so as if they were lost they could be recognized and brocht back."

"Certainly it is a scheme deserving consideration, and I have no doubt our geniuses would jump at it; but you must remember that some of them would have wives."

"Ay, an' some o' them would hae husbands. I've been thinkin' that oot, an' I daursay the best plan would be to partition aff a pairt o' the Home for female geniuses."

"Would Parliament elect the members?"

"I wouldna trust them. The election would hae to be by competitive examination. Na, I canna say wha would draw up the queistions. The scheme's juist growin' i' my mind, but the mair I think o't the better I like it."

Chapter 18

LEEBY AND JAMIE

By the bank of the Quharity on a summer day I have seen a barefooted girl gaze at the running water until tears filled her eyes. That was the birth of romance. Whether this love be but a beautiful dream I cannot say, but this we see, that it comes to all, and colours the whole future life with gold. Leeby must have dreamt it, but I did not know her then. I have heard of a man who would have taken her far away into a country where the corn is yellow when it is still green with us, but she would not leave her mother, nor was it him she saw in her dream. From her earliest days, when she was still a child staggering round the garden with Jamie in her arms, her duty lay before her, straight as the burying-ground road. Jess had need of her in the little home at the top of the brae, where God, looking down upon her as she scrubbed and gossipped and sat up all night with her ailing mother, and never missed the prayer-meeting, and adored the minister, did not perhaps think her the least of His handmaids. Her years were less than thirty when He took her away, but she had few days that were altogether dark. Those who bring sunshine to the lives of others cannot keep it from themselves.

The love Leeby bore for Jamie was such that in their younger days it shamed him. Other laddies knew of it, and flung it at him until he dared Leeby to let on in public that he and she were related.

"Hoo is your lass?" they used to cry to him, inventing a new game.

"I saw Leeby lookin' for ye," they would say; "she's wearyin' for ye to gang an' play wi' her."

Then if they were not much bigger boys than himself, Jamie got them against the dyke and hit them hard until they publicly owned to knowing that she was his sister, and that he was not fond of her.

"It distressed him mair than ye could believe, though," Jess has told me; "an' when he came hame he would greet an' say 'at Leeby disgraced him."

Leeby, of course, suffered for her too obvious affection.

"I wonder 'at ye dinna try to control yersel," Jamie would say to her, as he grew bigger.

" 'Am sure," said Leeby, "I never gie ye a look if there's onybody there."

"A look! You're aye lookin' at me sae fondlike 'at I dinna ken what wy to turn."

"Weel, I canna help it," said Leeby, probably beginning to whimper.

If Jamie was in a very bad temper he left her, after this, to her own reflections; but he was naturally softhearted.

" 'Am no tellin' ye no to care for me," he told her, "but juist to keep it mair to yersel. Naebody would ken frae me 'at 'am fond o' ye."

"Mebbe yer no?" said Leeby.

"Ay, am I, but I can keep it secret. When we're in the hoose am juist richt fond o' ye."

"Do ye love me, Jamie?"

Jamie waggled his head in irritation.

"Love," he said, "is an awful like word to use when fowk's weel. Ye shouldna speir sic annoyin' questions."

"But if ye juist say ye love me I'll never let on again afore fowk 'at yer onything to me ava."

"Ay, ye often say that."

"Do ye no believe my word?"

"I believe fine ye mean what ye say, but ye forget yersel when the time comes."

"Juist try me this time."

"Weel, then, I do."

"Do what?" asked the greedy Leeby.

"What ye said."

"I said love."

"Weel," said Jamie, " I do't."

"What do ye do? Say the word."

"Na," said Jamie, "I winna say the word. It's no a word to say, but I do't."

That was all she could get out of him, unless he was stricken with remorse, when he even went the length of saying the word.

"Leeby kent perfectly weel," Jess has said, " 'at it was a trial to Jamie to tak her ony gait, an' I often used to say to her 'at I wondered at her want o' pride in priggin' wi' him. Ay, but if she could juist get a promise wrung oot o' him, she didna care hoo muckle she had to prig. Syne they quarrelled, an' ane or baith o' them grat (cried) afore they made it up. I mind when Jamie went to the fishin' Leeby was aye terrible keen to get wi' him, but ye see he wouldna be seen gaen through the toon wi' her. 'If ye let me gang,' she said to him, 'I'll no seek to go through the toon wi' ye. Na, I'll gang roond by the Roods an' you can tak the buryin'-ground road, so as we can meet on the hill.' Yes, Leeby was willin' to agree wi' a' that juist to get gaen wi' him. I've seen lassies makkin' themsels sma' for lads often enough, but I never saw ane 'at prigged so muckle wi' her ain brother. Na, it's other lassies' brothers they like as a rule."

"But though Jamie was terrible reserved aboot it," said Leeby, "he was as fond o' me as ever I was o' him. Ye mind the time I had the measles, mother?"

" 'Am no likely to forget it, Leeby," said Jess, "an' you blind wi' them for three days. Ay, ay, Jamie was richt taen up aboot ye. I mind he broke open his pirly (money-box), an' bocht a ha'penny worth o' something to ye every day."

"An' ye hinna forgotten the stick?"

" 'Deed no, I hinna. Ye see," Jess explained to me, "Leeby was lyin' ben the hoose, an' Jamie wasna allowed to gang near her for fear o' infection. Weel, he got a lang stick—it was a peastick— an' put it 'aneath the door an' waggled it. Ay, he did that a curran times every day, juist to let her see he was thinkin' o' her."

"Mair than that," said Leeby, "he cried oot 'at he loved me."

"Ay, but juist aince," Jess said; "I dinna mind o't but aince. It was the time the doctor came late, an' Jamie, being waukened by him, thocht ye was deein'. I mind as if it was yesterday hoo he cam runnin' to the door an' cried oot, 'I do love ye, Leeby; I love ye richt.' The doctor got a start when he heard the voice, but he laughed loud when he unerstood."

"He had nae business, though," said Leeby, "to tell onybody."

"He was a rale clever man, the doctor," Jess explained to me; "ay, he kent me as weel as though he'd gaen through me wi' a lichted candle. It got oot through him, an' the young billies took to sayin' to Jamie, 'Ye do love her, Jamie; ay, ye love her richt.' The only reglar fecht I ever kent Jamie hae was wi' a lad 'at cried that to him. It was Bowlegs Christy's laddie. Ay, but when she got better Jamie blamed Leeby."

"He no only blamed me," said Leeby, "but he wanted me to pay him back a' the bawbees he had spent on me."

"Ay, an' I sepad he got them too," said Jess.

In time Jamie became a barber in Tilliedrum, trudging many heavy miles there and back twice a day that he might sleep at home, trudging bravely I was to say, but it was what he was born to, and there was hardly an alternative. This was the time I saw most of him, and he and Leeby were often in my thoughts. There is as terrible a bubble in the little kettle as on the cauldron of the world, and some of the scenes between Jamie and Leeby were great tragedies, comedies, what you will, until the kettle was taken off the fire. Hers was the more placid temper; indeed, only in one way could Jamie suddenly rouse her to fury. That was when he hinted that she had a large number of frocks. Leeby knew that there could never be more than a Sabbath frock and an everyday gown for her, both of her mother's making, but Jamie's insinuations were more than she could bear. Then I have seen her seize and shake him. I know from Jess that Leeby cried herself hoarse the day Joey was buried, because her little black frock was not ready for wear.

Until he went to Tilliedrum Jamie had been more a stay-at-home boy than most. The warmth of Jess's love had something to do with keeping his heart aglow, but more, I think, he owed to Leeby. Tilliedrum was his introduction to the world, and for a little it took his head. I was in the house the Sabbath day that he refused to go to church.

He went out in the forenoon to meet the Tilliedrum lads, who were to take him off for a holiday in a cart. Hendry was more wrathful than I remember ever to have seen him, though I have heard how he did with the lodger who broke the Lord's Day. This lodger was a tourist who thought, in folly surely rather than in hardness of heart, to test the religious convictions of an Auld Licht by insisting on paying his bill on a Sabbath morning. He offered the money to Jess, with the warning that if she did not take it now she might never see it. Jess was so kind and good to her lodgers that he could not have known her long who troubled her with this poor trick. She was sorely in need at the time, and entreated the thoughtless man to have some pity on her.

"Now or never," he said, holding out the money.

"Put it on the dresser," said Jess at last, "an' I'll get it the morn."

The few shillings were laid on the dresser, where they remained unfingered until Hendry, with Leeby and Jamie, came in from church.

"What siller's that?" asked Hendry, and then Jess confessed what she had done.

"I wonder at ye, woman," said Hendry, sternly; and lifting the money he climbed up to the attic with it.

He pushed open the door, and confronted the lodger.

"Take back yer siller," he said, laying it on the table, "an' leave my hoose. Man, you're a pitiable crittur to tak the chance, when I was oot, o' playin' upon the poverty o' an onweel woman."

It was with such unwonted severity as this that Hendry called upon Jamie to follow him to church; but the boy went off, and did not return till dusk, defiant and miserable. Jess had been so terrified that she forgave him everything for sight of his face, and Hendry prayed for him at family worship with too much unction. But Leeby cried as if her tender heart would break. For a long time Jamie refused to look at her, but at last he broke down.

"If ye go on like that," he said, "I'll gang awa oot an' droon mysel, or be a sojer."

This was no uncommon threat of his, and sometimes, when he went off, banging the door violently, she ran after him and brought him back. This time she only wept the more, and so both went to bed in misery. It was after midnight that Jamie rose and crept to Leeby's bedside. Leeby was shaking the bed in her agony. Jess heard what they said.

"Leeby," said Jamie, "dinna greet, an' I'll never do't again."

He put his arms round her, and she kissed him passionately.

"Oh, Jamie," she said, "hae ye prayed to God to forgie ye?"

Jamie did not speak.

"If ye was to die this nicht," cried Leeby, "an' you no made it up wi' God, ye wouldna gang to heaven. Jamie, I canna sleep till ye've made it up wi' God."

But Jamie still hung back. Leeby slipped from her bed, and went down on her knees.

"O God, O dear God," she cried, "mak Jamie to pray to you!"

Then Jamie went down on his knees too, and they made it up with God together.

This is a little thing for me to remember all these years, and yet how fresh and sweet it keeps Leeby in my memory.

Away up in the glen, my lonely schoolhouse lying deep, as one might say, in a sea of snow, I had many hours in the years long by for thinking of my friends in Thrums and mapping out the future of Leeby and Jamie. I saw Hendry and Jess taken to the churchyard and Leeby left alone in the house. I saw Jamie fulfil his promise to his mother, and take Leeby, that stainless young woman, far away to London, where they had a home together. Ah, but these were only the idle dreams of a dominie. The Lord willed it otherwise.

Chapter 19

A TALE OF A GLOVE

So long as Jamie was not the lad, Jess twinkled gleefully over tales of sweethearting. There was little Kitty Lamby who used to skip in of an evening, and, squatting on a stool near the window, unwind the roll of her enormities. A wheedling thing she was, with an ambition to drive men crazy, but my presence killed the gossip on her tongue, though I liked to look at her. When I entered, the wag-at-the-wa' clock had again possession of the kitchen. I never heard more than the end of a sentence:

"An' did he really say he would fling himsel into the dam, Kitty?"

Or— "True as death, Jess, he kissed me."

Then I wandered away from the kitchen, where I was not wanted, and marvelled to know that Jess of the tender heart laughed most merrily when he really did say that he was going straight to the dam. As no body was found in the dam in those days, whoever he was he must have thought better of it.

But let Kitty, or any other maid, cast a glinting eye on Jamie, then Jess no longer smiled. If he returned the glance she sat silent in her chair till Leeby laughed away her fears.

"Jamie's no the kind, mother," Leeby would say. "Na, he's quiet, but he sees through them. They dinna draw his leg (get over him)."

"Ye never can tell, Leeby. The laddies 'at's maist ill to get sometimes gangs up in a flame a' at aince, like a bit o' paper."

"Ay, weel, at ony rate Jamie's no on fire yet."

Though clever beyond her neighbours, Jess lost all her sharpness if they spoke of a lassie for Jamie.

"I warrant," Tibbie Birse said one day in my hearing, "'at there's some leddy in London he's thinkin' o'. Ay, he's been a guid laddie to ye, but i' the coorse o' nature he'll be settlin' dune soon."

Jess did not answer, but she was a picture of woe.

"Yer lettin' what Tibbie Birse said lie on yer mind," Leeby remarked, when Tibbie was gone. "What can it maiter what she thinks?"

"I canna help it, Leeby," said Jess. "Na, an' I canna bear to think o' Jamie bein' mairit. It would lay me low to loss my laddie. No yet, no yet."

"But, mother," said Leeby, quoting from the minister at weddings, "ye wouldna be lossin' a son, but juist gainin' a dochter."

"Dinna haver, Leeby," answered Jess, "I want nane o' thae dochters; na, na."

This talk took place while we were still awaiting Jamie's coming. He had only been with us one day when Jess made a terrible discovery. She was looking so mournful when I saw her, that I asked Leeby what was wrong.

"She's brocht it on hersel," said Leeby. "Ye see she was up sune i' the mornin' to begin to the darnin' o' Jamie's stockins an' to warm his sark at the fire afore he put it on. He woke up, an' cried to her 'at he wasna accustomed to ha'en his things warmed for him. Ay, he cried it oot fell thrawn, so she took it into her head 'at there was something in his pouch he didna want her to see. She was even onaisy last nicht."

I asked what had aroused Jess's suspicions last night.

"Ou, ye would notice 'at she sat devourin' him wi' her een, she was so lifted up at ha'en 'im again. Weel, she says noo 'at she saw 'im twa or three times put his hand in his pouch as if he was findin' to mak sure 'at something was safe. So when he fell asleep again this mornin' she got haud o' his jacket to see if there was onything in't. I advised her no to do't, but she couldna help hersel. She put in her hand, an' pu'd it oot. That's what's makkin' her look sae ill."

"But what was it she found?"

"Did I no tell ye? I'm ga'en dottle, I think. It was a glove, a woman's glove, in a bit paper. Ay, though she's sittin' still she's near frantic."

I said I supposed Jess had put the glove back in Jamie's pocket.

"Na," said Leeby, " 'deed no. She wanted to fling it on the back o' the fire, but I woudna let her. That's it she has aneath her apron."

Later in the day I remarked to Leeby that Jamie was very dull.

"He's missed it," she explained.

"Has any one mentioned it to him," I asked, "or has he inquired about it?"

"Na," said Leeby, "there hasna been a syllup (syllable) aboot it. My mother's fleid to mention't, an' he doesna like to speak aboot it either."

"Perhaps he thinks he has lost it?"

"Nae fear o' him," Leeby said. "Na, he kens fine wha has't."

I never knew how Jamie came by the glove, nor whether it had originally belonged to her who made him forget the window at the top of the brae. At the time I looked on as at play-acting, rejoicing in the happy ending. Alas! in the real life how are we to know when we have reached an end?

But this glove, I say, may not have been that woman's, and if it was, she had not then bedevilled him. He was too sheepish to demand it back from his mother, and already he cared for it too much to laugh at Jess's theft with Leeby. So it was that a curious game at chess was played with the glove, the players a silent pair.

Jamie cared little to read books, but on the day following Jess's discovery, I found him on his knees in the attic, looking through mine. A little box, without a lid, held them all, but they seemed a great library to him.

"There's readin' for a lifetime in them," he said. "I was juist takkin' a look through them."

His face was guilty, however, as if his hand had been caught in a money-bag, and I wondered what had enticed the lad to my books. I was still standing pondering when Leeby ran up the stair; she was so active that she generally ran, and she grudged the time lost in recovering her breath.

"I'll put yer books richt," she said, making her word good as she spoke. "I kent Jamie had been ransackin' up here, though he cam up rale canny. Ay, ye would notice he was in his stockin' soles."

I had not noticed this, but I remembered now his slipping from the room very softly. If he wanted a book, I told Leeby, he could have got it without any display of cunning.

"It's no a book he's lookin' for," she said, "na, it's his glove."

The time of day was early for Leeby to gossip, but I detained her for a moment.

"My mother's hodded (hid) it," she explained, "an' he winna speir nae queistions. But he's lookin' for't. He was ben in the room searchin' the drawers when I was up i' the toon in the forenoon. Ye see he pretends no to be carin' afore me, an' though my mother's sittin' sae quiet-like at the window she's hearkenin' a' the time. Ay, an' he thocht I had hod it up here."

But where, I asked, was the glove hid.

"I ken nae mair than yersel," said Leeby. "My mother's gi'en to hoddin' things. She has a place aneath the bed whaur she keeps the siller, an' she's no speakin' aboot the glove to me noo, because she thinks Jamie an' me's in comp (company). I speired at her whaur she had hod it, but she juist said, 'What would I be doin' hoddin't?' She'll never admit to me 'at she hods the siller either."

Next day Leeby came to me with the latest news.

"He's found it," she said, "ay, he's got the glove again. Ye see, what put him on the wrang scent was a notion 'at I had put it some gait. He kent 'at if she'd hod it, the kitchen maun be the place, but he thocht she'd gi'en it to me to hod. He cam upon't by accident. It was aneath the paddin' o' her chair."

Here, I thought, was the end of the glove incident, but I was mistaken. There were no presses or drawers with locks in the house, and Jess got hold of the glove again. I suppose she had reasoned out no line of action. She merely hated the thought that Jamie should have a woman's glove in his possession.

"She beats a' wi' 'cuteness," Leeby said to me. "Jamie didna put the glove back in his pouch. Na, he kens her ower weel by this time. She was up, though, lang afore he was wauken, an' she gaed almost strecht to the place whaur he had hod it. I believe she lay waukin a' nicht thinkin' oot whaur it would be. Ay, it was aneath the mattress. I saw her hodden't i' the back o' the drawer, but I didna let on."

I quite believed Leeby when she told me afterwards that she had watched Jamie feeling beneath the mattress.

"He had a face," she said, "I assure ye, he had a face, when he discovered the glove was gone again."

"He maun be terrible ta'en up aboot it," Jess said to Leeby, "or he wouldna keep it aneath the mattress."

"Od," said Leeby, " it was yersel 'at drove him to't."

Again Jamie recovered his property, and again Jess got hold of it. This time he looked in vain. I learnt the fate of the glove from Leeby.

"Ye mind 'at she keepit him at hame frae the kirk on Sabbath, because he had a cauld?" Leeby said. "Ay, me or my father would hae a gey ill cauld afore she would let's bide at hame frae the kirk; but Jamie's different. Weel, mair than aince she's been near speakin' to 'im aboot the glove, but she grew fleid aye. She was sae terrified there was something in't.

"On Sabbath, though, she had him to hersel, an' he wasna so bright as usual. She sat wi' the Bible on her lap, pretendin' to read, but a' the time she was takkin' keeks (glances) at him. I dinna ken 'at he was broodin' ower the glove, but she thocht he was, an' juist afore the kirk came oot she couldna stand it nae langer. She put her hand in her pouch, an' pu'd oot the glove, wi' the paper round it, juist as it had been when she came upon't.

" 'That's yours, Jamie,' she said; 'it was ill-dune o' me to tak it, but I couldna help it.'

"Jamie put oot his hand, an' syne he drew't back. 'It's no a thing o' nae consequence, mother,' he said.

" 'Wha is she, Jamie?' my mother said.

"He turned awa his heid—so she telt me. 'It's a lassie in London,' he said, 'I dinna ken her muckle.'

"'Ye maun ken her weel,' my mother persisted, 'to be carryin' aboot her glove; I'm dootin' yer gey fond o' her, Jamie?'

" 'Na', said Jamie, ' 'am no. There's no naebody I care for like yersel, mother.'

"'Ye wouldna carry aboot onything o' mine, Jamie,' my mother said; but he says, 'Oh, mother, I carry aboot yer face wi' me aye; an' sometimes at nicht I kind o' greet to think o' ye.'

"Ay, after that I've nae doot he was sittin' wi' his airms aboot her. She didna tell me that, but weel he kens it's what she likes, an' she maks nae pretence o' it's no bein'. But for a' he said an' did, she noticed him put the glove back in his inside pouch.

" 'It's wrang o' me, Jamie,' she said, 'but I canna bear to think o' ye carryin' that aboot sae carefu'. No, I canna help it.'

"Weel, Jamie, the crittur, took it oot o' his pouch, an' kind o' hesitated. Syne he lays't on the back o'the fire, an'they sat thegither glowerin' at it.

" 'Noo, mother,' he says, 'you're satisfied, are ye no?'

"Ay," Leeby ended her story, "she said she was satisfied. But she saw 'at he laid it on the fire fell fond-like."

Chapter 20

THE LAST NIGHT

"Juist another sax nichts, Jamie," Jess would say, sadly. "Juist fower nichts noo, an' you'll be awa." Even as she spoke seemed to come the last night.

The last night! Reserve slipped unheeded to the floor. Hendry wandered ben and but the house, and Jamie sat at the window holding his mother's hand. You must walk softly now if you would cross that humble threshold. I stop at the door. Then, as now, I was a lonely man, and when the last night came the attic was the place for me.

This family affection, how good and beautiful it is. Men and maids love, and after many years they may rise to this. It is the grand proof of the goodness in human nature, for it means that the more we see of each other the more we find that is lovable. If you would cease to dislike a man, try to get nearer his heart.

Leeby had no longer any excuse for bustling about. Everything was ready too soon. Hendry had been to the fish-cadger in the square to get a bervie for Jamie's supper, and Jamie had eaten it, trying to look as if it made him happier. His little box was packed and strapped, and stood terribly conspicuous against the dresser. Jess had packed it herself.

"Ye mauna trachle (trouble) yersel, mother," Jamie said, when she had the empty box pulled toward her.

Leeby was wiser.

"Let her do't," she whispered, "it'll keep her frae broodin'."

Jess tied ends of yarn round the stockings to keep them in a little bundle by themselves. So she did with all the other articles.

"No 'at it's ony great affair," she said, for on the last night they were all thirsting to do something for Jamie that would be a great affair to him.

"Ah, ye would wonder, mother," Jamie said, "when I open my box an' find a'thing tied up wi' strings sae carefu', it a' comes back to me wi' a rush wha did it, an' 'am as fond o' thae strings as though they were a grand present. There's the pocky (bag) ye gae me to keep sewin' things in. I get the wifie I lodge wi' to sew to me, but often when I come upon the pocky I sit an' look at it."

Two chairs were backed to the fire, with underclothing hanging upside down on them. From the string over the fireplace dangled two pairs of much-darned stockings.

"Ye'll put on baith thae pair o'stockin's, Jamie," said Jess, "juist to please me?"

When he arrived he had rebelled against the extra clothing.

"Ay, will I, mother?" he said now.

Jess put her hand fondly through his ugly hair. How handsome she thought him.

"Ye have a fine brow, Jamie," she said. "I mind the day ye was born sayin' to mysel 'at ye had a fine brow."

"But ye thocht he was to be a lassie, mother," said Leeby.

"Na, Leeby, I didna. I kept sayin' I thocht he would be a lassie because I was fleid he would be; but a' the time I had a presentiment he would be a laddie. It was wi' Joey deein' sae sudden, an' I took on sae terrible aboot 'im 'at I thocht a' alang the Lord would gie me another laddie."

"Ay, I wanted 'im to be a laddie mysel," said Hendry, "so as he could tak Joey's place."

Jess's head jerked back involuntarily, and Jamie may have felt her hand shake, for he said in a voice out of Hendry's hearing —

"I never took Joey's place wi' ye, mother."

Jess pressed his hand tightly in her two worn palms, but she did not speak.

"Jamie was richt like Joey when he was a bairn," Hendry said.

Again Jess's head moved, but still she was silent.

"They were sae like," continued Hendry, " 'at often I called Jamie by Joey's name."

Jess looked at her husband, and her mouth opened and shut.

"I canna mind 'at ye ever did that?" Hendry said.

She shook her head.

"Na," said Hendry, "you never mixed them up. I dinna think ye ever missed Joey sae sair as I did."

Leeby went ben, and stood in the room in the dark; Jamie knew why.

"I'll just gang ben an' speak to Leeby for a meenute," he said to his mother; "I'll no be lang."

"Ay, do that, Jamie," said Jess. "What Leeby's been to me nae tongue can tell. Ye canna bear to hear me speak, I ken, o' the time when Hendry an' me 'll be awa, but, Jamie, when that time comes ye'll no forget Leeby?"

"I winna, mother, I winna," said Jamie. "There'll never be a roof ower me 'at's no hers too."

He went ben and shut the door. I do not know what he and Leeby said. Many a time since their earliest youth had these two been closeted together, often to make up their little quarrels in each other's arms. They remained a long time in the room, the shabby room of which Jess and Leeby were so proud, and whatever might be their fears about their mother they were not anxious for themselves.

Leeby was feeling lusty and well, and she could not know that Jamie required to be reminded of his duty to the folk at home. Jamie would have laughed at the notion. Yet that woman in London must have been waiting for him even then. Leeby, who was about to die, and Jamie, who was to forget his mother, came back to the kitchen with a happy light on their faces. I have with me still the look of love they gave each other before Jamie crossed over to Jess.

"Ye'll gang anower, noo, mother," Leeby said, meaning that it was Jess's bed-time.

"No yet, Leeby," Jess answered, "I'll sit up till the readin's ower."

"I think ye should gang, mother," Jamie said, an' I'll come an' sit aside ye after ye're i' yer bed."

"Ay, Jamie, I'll no hae ye to sit aside me the morn's nicht, an' hap (cover) me wi' the claes."

"But ye'll gang suner to yer bed, mother."

"I may gang, but I winna sleep. I'll aye be thinkin' o' ye tossin' on the sea. I pray for ye a lang time ilka nicht, Jamie."

"Ay, I ken."

"An' I pictur ye ilka hour o' the day. Ye never gang hame through thae terrible streets at nicht but I'm thinkin' o' ye."

"I would try no to be sae sad, mother," said Leeby. "We've ha'en a richt fine time, have we no?"

"It's been an awfu' happy time," said Jess. "We've ha'en a pleasantness in oor lives 'at comes to few. I ken naebody 'at's ha'en sae muckle happiness one wy or another."

"It's because ye're sae guid, mother," said Jamie.

"Na, Jamie, 'am no guid ava. It's because my fowk's been sae guid, you an' Hendry an' Leeby an' Joey when he was livin'. I've got a lot mair than my deserts."

"We'll juist look to meetin' next year again, mother. To think o' that keeps me up a' the winter."

"Ay, if it's the Lord's will, Jamie, but 'am gey dune noo, an' Hendry's fell worn too."

Jamie, the boy that he was, said, "Dinna speak like that, mother," and Jess again put her hand on his head.

"Fine I ken, Jamie," she said, " 'at all my days on this earth, be they short or lang, I've you for a staff to lean on."

Ah, many years have gone since then, but if Jamie be living now he has still those words to swallow.

By and by Leeby went ben for the Bible, and put it into Hendry's hands. He slowly turned over the leaves to his favourite chapter, the fourteenth of John's Gospel. Always, on eventful occasions, did Hendry turn to the fourteenth of John.

"Let not your heart be troubled; ye believe in God, believe also in Me.

"In My Father's house are many mansions; if it were not so I would' have told you. I go to prepare a place for you."

As Hendry raised his voice to read there was a great stillness in the kitchen. I do not know that I have been able to show in the most imperfect way what kind of man Hendry was. He was dense in many things, and the cleverness that was Jess's had been denied to him. He had less book-learning than most of those with whom he passed his days, and he had little skill in talk. I have not known a man more easily taken in by persons whose speech had two faces. But a more simple, modest, upright man there never was in Thrums, and I shall always revere his memory.

"And if I go and prepare a place for you, I will come again, and receive you unto Myself; that where I am there ye may be also."

The voice may have been monotonous. I have always thought that Hendry's reading of the Bible was the most solemn and impressive I have ever heard. He exulted in the fourteenth of John, pouring it forth like one whom it intoxicated while he read. He emphasized every other word; it was so real and grand to him.

We went upon our knees while Hendry prayed, all but Jess, who could not. Jamie buried his face in her lap. The words Hendry said were those he used every night. Some, perhaps, would have smiled at his prayer to God that we be not puffed up with riches nor with the things of this world. His head shook with emotion while he prayed, and he brought us very near to the throne of grace. "Do thou, O our God," he said, in conclusion, "spread Thy guiding hand over him whom in Thy great mercy Thou hast brought to us again, and do Thou guard him through the perils which come unto those that go down to the sea in ships. Let not our hearts be troubled, neither let them be afraid, for this is not our abiding home, and may we all meet in Thy house, where there are many mansions, and where there will be no last night. Amen."

It was a silent kitchen after that, though the lamp burned long in Jess's window. By its meagre light you may take a final glance at the little family; you will never see them together again.

Chapter 21

JESS LEFT ALONE

There may be a few who care to know how the lives of Jess and Hendry ended. Leeby died in the back-end of the year I have been speaking of, and as I was snowed up in the school-house at the time, I heard the news from Gavin Birse too late to attend her funeral. She got her death on the commonty one day of sudden rain, when she had run out to bring in her washing, for the terrible cold she woke with next morning carried her off very quickly. Leeby did not blame Jamie for not coming to her, nor did I, for I knew that even in the presence of death the poor must drag their chains. He never got Hendry's letter with the news, and we know now that he was already in the hands of her who played the devil with his life. Before the spring came he had been lost to Jess.

"Them 'at has got sae mony blessin's mair than the generality," Hendry said to me one day, when Craigiebuckle had given me a lift into Thrums, "has nae shame if they would pray aye for mair. The Lord has gi'en this hoose sae muckle, 'at to pray for mair looks like no bein' thankfu' for what we've got. Ay, but I canna help prayin' to Him 'at in His great mercy he'll tak Jess afore me. Noo 'at Leeby's gone, an' Jamie never lets us hear frae him, I canna gulp doon the thocht o' Jess bein' left alane."

This was a prayer that Hendry may be pardoned for having so often in his heart, though God did not think fit to grant it. In Thrums, when a weaver died, his womenfolk had to take his seat at the loom, and those who, by reason of infirmities, could not do so, went to a place, the name of which, I thank God, I am not compelled to write in this chapter. I could not, even at this day, have told any episodes in the life of Jess had it ended in the poorhouse.

Hendry would probably have recovered from the fever had not this terrible dread darkened his intellect when he was still prostrate. He was lying in the kitchen when I saw him last in life, and his parting words must be sadder to the reader than they were to me.

"Ay, richt ye are," he said, in a voice that had become a child's; "I hae muckle, muckle, to be thankfu' for, an' no the least is 'at baith me an' Jess has aye belonged to a bural society. We hae nae cause to be anxious aboot a' thing bein' dune respectable aince we're gone. It was Jess 'at insisted on oor joinin': a' the wisest things I ever did I was put up to by her."

I parted from Hendry, cheered by the doctor's report, but the old weaver died a few days afterwards. His end was mournful, yet I can recall it now as the not unworthy close of a good man's life. One night poor worn Jess had been helped ben into the room, Tibbie Birse having undertaken to sit up with Hendry. Jess slept for the first time for many days, and as the night was dying Tibbie fell asleep too. Hendry had been better than usual, lying quietly, Tibbie said, and the fever was gone. About three o'clock Tibbie woke and rose to mend the fire. Then she saw that Hendry was not in his bed.

Tibbie went ben the house in her stocking-soles, but Jess heard her.

"What is't, Tibbie?" she asked, anxiously.

"Ou, it's no naething," Tibbie said, "he's lyin' rale quiet."

Then she went up to the attic. Hendry was not in the house.

She opened the door gently and stole out. It was not snowing, but there had been a heavy fall two days before, and the night was windy. A tearing gale had blown the upper part of the brae clear, and from T'nowhead's fields the snow was rising like smoke. Tibbie ran to the farm and woke up T'nowhead.

For an hour they looked in vain for Hendry. At last some one asked who was working in Elshioner's shop all night. This was the long earthen-floored room in which Hendry's loom stood with three others.

"It'll be Sanders Whamond likely," T'nowhead said, and the

other men nodded.

But it happened that T'nowhead's Bell, who had flung on a wrapper, and hastened across to sit with Jess, heard of the light in Elshioner's shop.

"It's Hendry," she cried, and then every one moved toward the workshop.

The light at the diminutive, yarn-covered window was pale and dim, but Bell, who was at the house first, could make the most of a cruizey's glimmer.

"It's him," she said, and then, with swelling throat, she ran back to Jess.

The door of the workshop was wide open, held against the wall by the wind. T'nowhead and the others went in. The cruizey stood on the little window. Hendry's back was to the door, and he was leaning forward on the silent loom. He had been dead for some time, but his fellow-workers saw that he must have weaved for nearly an hour.

So it came about that for the last few months of her pilgrimage Jess was left alone. Yet I may not say that she was alone. Jamie, who should have been with her, was undergoing his own ordeal far away; where, we did not now even know. But though the poorhouse stands in Thrums, where all may see it, the neighbours did not think only of themselves.

Than Tammas Haggart there can scarcely have been a poorer man, but Tammas was the first to come forward with offer of help. To the day of Jess's death he did not once fail to carry her water to her in the morning, and the luxuriously living men of Thrums in those present days of pumps at every corner can hardly realize what that meant. Often, there were lines of people at the well by three o'clock in the morning, and each had to wait his turn. Tammas filled his own pitcher and pan, and then had to take his place at the end of the line with Jess's pitcher and pan, to wait his turn again. His own house was in the Tenements, far from the brae in winter time, but he always said to Jess it was "naething ava."

Every Saturday old Robbie Angus sent a bag of sticks and

shavings from the saw-mill by his little son Rob, who was afterwards to become a man for speaking about at nights. Of all the friends that Jess and Hendry had, T'nowhead was the ablest to help, and the sweetest memory I have of the farmer and his wife is the delicate way they offered it. You who read will see Jess wince at the offer of charity. But the poor have fine feelings beneath the grime, as you will discover if you care to look for them, and when Jess said she would bake if any one would buy, you would wonder to hear how many kindly folk came to her door for scones.

She had the house to herself at nights, but Tibbie Birse was with her early in the morning, and other neighbours dropped in. Not for long did she have to wait the summons to the better home.

"Na," she said to the minister, who has told me that he was a better man from knowing her, "my thochts is no nane set on the vanities o' the world noo. I kenna hoo I could ever hae ha'en sic an ambeetion to hae thae stuff-bottomed chairs."

I have tried to keep away from Jamie, whom the neighbours sometimes upbraided in her presence. It is of him you who read would like to hear, and I cannot pretend that Jess did not sit at her window looking for him.

"Even when she was bakin'," Tibbie told me, "she aye had an eye on the brae. If Jamie had come at ony time when it was licht she would hae seen 'im as sune as he turned the corner."

"If he ever comes back, the sacket (rascal)," T'nowhead said to Jess, "we'll show 'im the door gey quick."

Jess just looked, and all the women knew how she would take Jamie to her arms.

We did not know of the London woman then, and Jess never knew of her. Jamie's mother never for an hour allowed that he had become anything but the loving laddie of his youth.

"I ken 'im ower weel," she always said, "my ain Jamie."

Toward the end she was sure he was dead. I do not know when she first made up her mind to this, nor whether it was not merely a phrase for those who wanted to discuss him with her. I know that she still sat at the window looking at the elbow of the brae.

The minister was with her when she died. She was in her chair, and he asked her, as was his custom, if there was any particular chapter which she would like him to read. Since her husband's death she had always asked for the fourteenth of John, "Hendry's chapter," as it is still called among a very few old people in Thrums. This time she asked him to read the sixteenth chapter of Genesis.

"When I came to the thirteenth verse," the minister told me, "'And she called the name of the Lord that spake unto her, Thou God seest me,' she covered her face with her two hands, and said, 'Joey's text, Joey's text. Oh, but I grudged ye sair, Joey.'"

"I shut the book," the minister said, "when I came to the end of the chapter, and then I saw that she was dead. It is my belief that her heart broke one-and-twenty years ago."

Chapter 22

JAMIE'S HOME-COMING

On a summer day, when the sun was in the weavers' workshops, and bairns hopped solemnly at the game of palaulays, or gaily shook their bottles of sugarelly water into a froth, Jamie came back. The first man to see him was Hookey Crewe, the post.

"When he came frae London," Hookey said afterwards at T'nowhead's pig-sty, "Jamie used to wait for me at Zoar, i' the north end o' Tilliedrum. He carried his box ower the market muir, an' sat on't at Zoar, waitin' for me to catch 'im up. Ay, the day afore yesterday me an' the powny was clatterin' by Zoar, when there was Jamie standin' in his identical place. He hadna nae box to sit upon, an' he was far frae bein' weel in order, but I kent 'im at aince, an' I saw 'at he was waitin' for me. So I drew up, an' waved my hand to 'im."

"I would hae drove straucht by 'im," said T'nowhead; "them 'at leaves their auld mother to want doesna deserve a lift."

"Ay, ye say that sittin' there," Hockey said "but, lads, I saw his face, an' as sure as death it was sic an' awfu' meeserable face 'at I couldna but pu' the powny up. Weel, he stood for the space o' a meenute lookin' straucht at me, as if he would like to come forrit but dauredna, an' syne he turned an' strided awa ower the muir like a huntit thing. I sat still i' the cart, an' when he was far awa he stoppit an' lookit again, but a' my cryin' wouldna bring him a step back, an' i' the end I drove on. I've thocht since syne 'at he didna ken whether his fowk was livin' or deid, an' was fleid to speir."

"He didna ken," said T'nowhead, "but the faut was his ain. It's ower late to be ta'en up aboot Jess noo."

"Ay, ay, T'nowhead," said Hookey, "it's aisy to you to speak like that. Ye didna see his face."

It is believed that Jamie walked from Tilliedrum, though no one is known to have met him on the road. Some two hours after the post left him he was seen by old Rob Angus at the sawmill.

"I was sawin' awa wi' a' my micht," Rob said, "an' little Rob was haudin' the booards, for they were silly but things, when something made me look at the window. It couldna hae been a tap on't, for the birds has used me to that, an' it would hardly be a shadow, for little Rob didna look up. Whatever it was I stoppit i' the middle o' a booard, an' lookit up, an' there I saw Jamie McQumpha. He joukit back when our een met, but I saw him weel; ay, it's a queer thing to say, but he had the face o'a man'at had come straucht frae hell."

"I stood starin' at the window," Angus continued, "after he'd gone, an' Robbie cried oot to ken what was the maiter wi' me. Ay, that brocht me back to mysel, an' I hurried oot to look for Jamie, but he wasna to be seen. That face gae me a turn."

From the saw-mill to the house at the top of the brae, some may remember, the road is up the commonty. I do not think any one saw Jamie on the commonty, though there were those to say they met him.

"He gae me sic a look," a woman said, " 'at I was fleid an' ran hame," but she did not tell the story until Jamie's home-coming had become a legend.

There were many women hanging out their washing on the commonty that day, and none of them saw him. I think Jamie must have approached his old home by the fields, and probably he held back until gloaming.

The young woman who was now mistress of the house at the top of the brae both saw and spoke with Jamie.

"Twa or three times," she said, "I had seen a man walk quick up the brae an' by the door. It was gettin' dark, but I noticed 'at he was short an' thin, an' I would hae said he wasna nane weel if it hadna been 'at he gaed by at sic a steek. He didna look our wy—at least no when he was close up, an' I set 'im doon for some ga'en aboot body. Na, I saw naething aboot 'im to be fleid at.

"The aucht o'clock bell was ringin' when I saw 'im to speak to. My twa-year-auld bairn was standin' aboot the door, an' I was makkin' some porridge for my man's supper when I heard the bairny skirlin'. She cam runnin' in to the hoose an' hung i' my wrapper, an' she was hingin' there, when I gaed to the door to see what was wrang.

"It was the man I'd seen passin' the hoose. He was standin' at the gate, which, as a'body kens, is but sax steps frae the hoose, an' I wondered at 'im neither runnin' awa nor comin' forrit. I speired at 'im what he meant by terrifyin' a bairn, but he didna say naething. He juist stood. It was ower dark to see his face richt, an' I wasna nane ta'en aback yet, no till he spoke. Oh, but he had a fearsome word when he did speak. It was a kind o' like a man hoarse wi' a cauld, an' yet no that either."

"'Wha bides i' this hoose?' he said, ay standin' there.

"'It's Davit Patullo's hoose,' I said, 'an' 'am the wife.'

"'Whaur's Hendry McQumpha?' he speired.

"'He's deid,' I said.

" He stood still for a fell while.

"'An' his wife, Jess?' he said.

"'She's deid, too,' I said.

"I thocht he gae a groan, but it may hae been the gate.

"'There was a dochter, Leeby?' he said.

"'Ay,' I said, 'she was ta'en first.'

"I saw 'im put up his hands to his face, an' he cried oot, 'Leeby too!' an' syne he kind o' fell agin the dyke. I never kent 'im nor nane o' his fowk, but I had heard aboot them, an' I saw 'at it would be the son frae London. It wasna for me to judge 'im, an' I said to 'im would he no come in by an' tak a rest. I was nearer 'im by that time, an' it's an awfu' haver to say 'at he had a face to frichten fowk. It was a rale guid face, but no ava what a body would like to see on a young man. I felt mair like greetin' mysel when I saw his face than drawin' awa frae 'im.

"But he wouldnae come in. 'Rest,' he said, like ane speakin' to 'imsel, 'na, there's nae mair rest for me.' I didna weel ken what mair to say to 'im, for he aye stood on, an' I wasna even sure 'at he saw me. He raised his heid when he heard me tellin' the bairn no to tear my wrapper.

" 'Dinna set yer heart ower muckle on that bairn,' he cried oot, sharp like. 'I was aince like her, an' I used to hing aboot my mother, too, in that very roady. Ay, I thocht I was fond o' her, an' she thocht it too. Tak' a care, wuman, 'at that bairn doesna grow up to murder ye.'

"He gae a lauch when he saw me tak haud o' the bairn, an' syne a' at ance he gaed awa quick. But he wasna far doon the brae when he turned an' came back.

" 'Ye'll, mebbe, tell me,' he said, richt low, 'if ye hae the furniture 'at used to be my mother's?'

" 'Na,' I said, 'it was roupit, an' I kenna whaur the things gaed, for me 'an my man comes frae Tilliedrum.'

" 'Ye wouldna hae heard,' he said, 'wha got the muckle airm-chair 'at used to sit i' the kitchen i' the window 'at looks ower the brae?'

" 'I couldna be sure,' I said, 'but there was an armchair 'at gaed to Tibbie Birse. If it was the ane ye mean, it a' gaed to bits, an' I think they burned it. It was gey dune.'

" 'Ay,' he said, 'it was gey dune.'

" 'There was the chairs ben i' the room,' he said, after a while.

"I said I thocht Sanders Elshioner had got them at a bargain because twa o' them was mended wi' glue, an' gey silly.

" 'Ay, that's them,' he said, 'they were richt neat mended. It was my mother 'at glued them. I mind o' her makkin' the glue, an' warnin' me an' my father no to sit on them. There was the clock too, an' the stool 'at my mother got oot an' into her bed wi', an' the basket 'at Leeby carried when she gaed the errands. The straw was aff the handle, an' my father mended it wi' strings.'

" 'I dinna ken,' I said, 'whaur nane o' thae gaed; but did yer mother hae a staff?'

" 'A little staff,' he said; 'it was near black wi' age. She couldna gang frae the bed to her chair withoot it. It was broadened oot at the foot wi' her leanin' on't sae muckle.'

"'I've heard tell,' I said, 'at the dominie up i' Glen Quharity took awa the staff.'

"He didna speir for nae other thing. He had the gate in his hand, but I dinna think he kent 'at he was swingin't back an' forrit. At last he let it go.

"'That's a',' he said, 'I maun awa. Good-nicht, an' thank ye kindly.'

"I watched 'im till he gaed oot o' sicht. He gaed doon the brae."

We learnt afterwards from the gravedigger that some one spent great part of that night in the graveyard, and we believe it to have been Jamie. He walked up the glen to the school-house next forenoon, and I went out to meet him when I saw him coming down the path.

"Ay," he said, " it's me come back."

I wanted to take him into the house and speak with him of his mother, but he would not cross the threshold.

"I cam oot," he said, "to see if ye would gie me her staff—no 'at I deserve't."

I brought out the staff and handed it to him, thinking that he and I would soon meet again. As he took it I saw that his eyes were sunk back into his head. Two great tears hung on his eyelids, and his mouth closed in agony. He stared at me till the tears fell upon his cheeks, and then he went away.

That evening he was seen by many persons crossing the square. He went up the brae to his old home, and asked leave to go through the house for the last time. First he climbed up into the attic, and stood looking in, his feet still on the stair. Then he came down and stood at the door of the room, but he went into the kitchen.

"I'll ask one last favour o' ye," he said to the woman; "I would like ye to leave me here alane for juist a little while."

"I gaed oot," the woman said "meanin' to leave 'im to 'imsel', but my bairnie wouldna come, an' he said, 'Never mind her,' so I left her wi' 'im an' closed the door. He was in a lang time, but I never kent what he did, for the bairn juist aye greets when I speir at her.

"I watched 'im frae the corner window gang doon the brae till he cam to the corner. I thocht he turned round there an' stood lookin' at the hoose. He would see me better than I saw him, for my lamp was i' the window, whaur I've heard tell his mother keepit her cruizey. When my man came in I speired at 'im if he'd seen onybody standin' at the corner o' the brae, an' he said he thocht he'd seen somebody wi' a little staff in his hand. Davit gaed doon to see if he was aye there after supper-time, but he was gone."

Jamie was never again seen in Thrums.

————————————————

As this book was going to print, Hutchinson published Lisa Chaney's *Hide-and-Seek with Angels: A Life of J. M. Barrie* (London, 2005). It is a profusely illustrated biography which gives a good insight into the background of the stories.

————————————————